P9-DXJ-690

THE BiRTHDAY BLASTOFF

THE BiRTHDAY BLASTOFF

DR. KATE BIBERDORF
WITH HILLARY HOMZIE

Philomel Books

Hi! My Name is Dr. Kate Biberdorf,

but most people call me Kate the Chemist. I perform explosive science experiments on national TV when I'm not in Austin, Texas, teaching chemistry classes. Besides being the best science in the entire world, chemistry is the study of energy and matter, and their interactions with each other. Like how I can use cornstarch and liquid bandage to make fake tattoos or baking soda and vinegar to power a rocket! If you read *The Birthday Blastoff* carefully, you will see how Little Kate the Chemist uses chemistry to solve problems in her everyday life.

But remember, none of the experiments in this book should be done without the supervision of a trained professional! If you are looking for some fun, safe, at-home experiments, check out my companion books, *Kate the Chemist: The Big Book of Experiments* and *Kate the Chemist: The Awesome Book of Edible Experiments for Kids*. (I've included one experiment in the back of this book—how to make a double balloon rocket!)

And one more thing: Science is all about making predictions (or forming hypotheses), which you can do right now! Will Little Kate the Chemist be able to use her science skills to find a way to be in two different places at once? Let's find out—it's time for Kate the Chemist's fourth adventure.

XOXO,
Kate

PHILOMEL BOOKS
An imprint of Penguin Random House LLC, New York

First published in the United States of America by Philomel Books,
an imprint of Penguin Random House LLC, 2021.

Philomel Books is a registered trademark of Penguin Random House LLC.

Penguin Books & colophon are registered trademarks of Penguin Books
Limited.

Visit us online at penguinrandomhouse.com.

Library of Congress Cataloging-in-Publication Data is available.

Printed in the USA

ISBN 9780593116647

1 3 5 7 9 10 8 6 4 2

Edited by Jill Santopolo. Designed by Lori Thorn.
Text set in ITC Stone Serif.

This book is a work of fiction. Any references to historical events, real people,
or real places are used fictitiously. Other names, characters, places, and
events are products of the author's imagination, and any resemblance to
actual events or places or persons, living or dead, is entirely coincidental.

The publisher does not have any control over and does not assume any
responsibility for author or third-party websites or their content.

Behind every young child
who believes in herself
is a parent or guardian
who believed in her first.
This book is dedicated to all
caregivers, and one in particular,
my mom, Teresa.

TABLE OF CONTENTS

CHAPTER ONE: A Black Hole **1**

CHAPTER TWO: An Educated Guess **7**

CHAPTER THREE: Twinsies! **13**

CHAPTER FOUR: A Space-Filled Day **21**

CHAPTER FIVE: The Bad Luck Kid **26**

CHAPTER SIX: Seeing Is Believing **30**

CHAPTER SEVEN: Getting Energized **36**

CHAPTER EIGHT: The Right Stuff **43**

CHAPTER NINE: The Proposal **51**

CHAPTER TEN: Looking for Answers **58**

CHAPTER ELEVEN: Something to Do with Pressure **62**

CHAPTER TWELVE: Getting Launched **66**

CHAPTER THIRTEEN: Things Are Getting Heavy **71**

CHAPTER FOURTEEN: Looking for a Solution **77**

CHAPTER FIFTEEN: Liam's Comet **85**

CHAPTER SIXTEEN: Blastoff! **90**

CHAPTER SEVENTEEN: Bad Atmosphere **97**

CHAPTER EIGHTEEN: Empty-Handed **102**

CHAPTER NINETEEN: Hot and Cold **109**

CHAPTER TWENTY: Something Sweet **121**

CHAPTER ONE

A BLACK HOLE

Observation (noun). In science, this means gaining knowledge about anything around you through your senses. For instance, you could observe the smell of cheese coming from the school cafeteria (and figure out that there's going to be pizza for lunch!).

I HAD TO KNOW what was inside the mystery box.

Outside the science lab a snowblower roared. The room filled with chatter. Everyone was whispering about the box sitting on a table in the middle of the room.

"I'm going to peek," I whispered.

Birdie Bhatt, my very best friend, jumped in front of me. "Don't even think about it, Kate."

"But . . . but . . ." The box was

wrapped in shiny tinfoil like a present. Only instead of a bow, there was a giant red question mark made of construction paper.

"Ms. Daly is right there." Birdie pointed to our after-school science club advisor, who stood at the doorway, welcoming kids.

I bit my fingernails. "I hate waiting."

"I know." Birdie smiled and her brown eyes crinkled. She knew me soooo well.

"Here." Birdie dug into her flower-covered backpack and handed me a caramel apple granola bar.

It was my favorite.

"Here." I unzipped a front compartment in my backpack and yanked out a bag of trail mix with M&M's and sunflower seeds.

"I love those," said Birdie in a hushed voice.

"I know." Now it was my turn to smile.

That's when Ms. Daly marched to the front of the class. She glanced up at the clock. Three fifteen exactly. She's a retired air force flight engineer and always starts on time. She says you can't keep fighter pilots waiting.

Of course, we weren't pilots. We were students at Rosalind Franklin Elementary School. Which is named for Dr. Rosalind Franklin, one of the greatest chemists of all time. Science is extra *extra* special at our school, which is just fine by me.

Ms. Daly clapped her hands. "Okay, folks. It's mystery box time!"

A bunch of kids made happy shrieks, and I whooped.

"We're going to work on your abilities to observe using your senses," continued Ms. Daly. "Give me some words to describe this box."

"It's got six sides," said Elijah Williams, who's one of my closest friends and also my next-door neighbor.

"It's a cube," I said.

"It's very pretty," added Birdie.

"That might be true, but that's how you feel about it," admitted Ms. Daly. "Give me a pure observation."

Birdie's blush spread to her ears. "It's silver," she murmured.

"And shiny!" I exclaimed.

"And all taped up so we can't see what's inside," groaned Steven McFee, a fourth grader wearing a basketball shirt.

"Perfect!" Ms. Daly grabbed a yellow pad. On it, she had written *facts* in black ink. "In science, we stick to facts. For example, we know that the moon has had enough to eat when it's full."

For a minute, nobody said anything. And then a few kids like me started grinning when we realized it was just her typical corny humor.

"Facts are observations about the world," continued Ms. Daly. "Like that your heart pumps blood. The sun comes out during the day. And there are seven beakers sitting on my desk."

"And today is Friday, November twenty-eighth, our weekly science club meeting," I called out. I think science is the best thing in the entire world. That's not an observation, it's a feeling. And it's a really good one!

"That's a fact, Kate," said Ms. Daly. "So, in addition to shape, we can pay attention to texture and sound." She gently shook the box. "And smell."

Tilting his chin, Memito Alvarez sniffed. "Hey! I smell something sweet." He rubbed his belly. "It's definitely candy." He popped out of his seat. "Is it candy?"

"Sorry, but no." Ms. Daly shook her head and not one short gray hair moved. She continued on with her lesson. "Scientists know things exist without even seeing them. All based on observations and evidence."

"Like dinosaurs?" piped up Elijah. "I saw a Tyrannosaurus fossil in a natural history museum, but no human being has ever seen a real T. rex."

Memito roared like a dinosaur. Birdie and I jerked back in surprise, and then giggled.

"There's something else scientists know based on evidence." In the back, a new girl with wavy pigtails raised her hand. I recognized her from the main office this morning, when she had come in with her dad to transfer to our school. "How about black holes?" she said. "You can't see them, but you know they exist."

"Oh, that's perfect, Tala!" I exclaimed.

"How do you know my name?" She didn't sound angry, just surprised.

"Kate is a psychic," joked Elijah, pressing his finger to his forehead. "That's how she knows all the answers. And names."

"Ha ha." I kicked the back of his chair. "I just overheard someone say it. Tala Campo. Down in the office."

"Kate's mom is *the principal*," explained Avery Cooper, which sounded like a brag.

Ugh. Now it was my turn to blush. I really don't like it when people make a fuss about who my mom is. "It's no big deal."

"Well, welcome, Tala," said Ms. Daly. "You seem to know a lot about astronomy. Anything else you want to share about black holes?"

Tala blew on her thick bangs. "The gravitational field of a black hole pulls nearby stars. Scientists can see the effect on the stars but not the hole itself."

"That's so cool!" I gushed, thinking about how in chemistry, scientists can't actually see super-small particles like electrons, but they know about them because of intricate experiments in the lab.

Ms. Daly leaned over the mystery box. "Okay, are you ready to see what's inside?"

"Oh yes!" My legs bounced. My thoughts bounced. I couldn't wait.

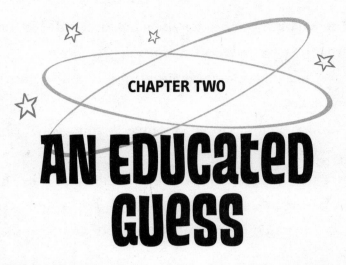

CHAPTER TWO

AN EDUCATED GUESS

Flash freeze (verb). When objects are frozen pretty much right away, often by direct contact with liquid nitrogen, which is extremely cold and which you should never ever touch. You don't ever want to flash freeze your brother, but it's great to flash freeze food, especially ice cream!

MS. DALY SET HER HANDS on the sides of the mystery box.

"O-pen it! O-pen it!" some boys chanted in the back of the room.

"Sure thing," said Ms. Daly. With a grunt, she heaved the box over her head. "Phew, it's heavy." With a wink, she set it down. "Just making sure everything's still in there. Plus, I want to torture you kids a little longer." Lifting the flaps, Ms. Daly opened up the carton.

With a big grin, she lifted out a yellow tub of cornstarch.

"Told you it was food!" shouted Memito, waving his finger.

"Dude, you said it was candy." Elijah elbowed his table partner.

"Cornstarch is used in lots of experiments," I said. "Even non-food ones."

"Not sure how you can be good observers if you're talking all at once." Ms. Daly tapped her foot.

"Oops! Sorry!" Sometimes when I'm super excited, I get a little hyper. With a wave of my arm, I zipped my lips.

Next Ms. Daly pulled out a glass jar of green powder.

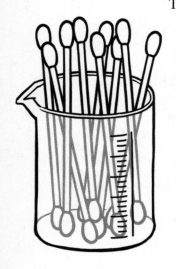

Then a jar of liquid bandage, alcohol pads, bowls, spoons, a package of cotton swabs, and beakers. Honestly, it didn't make sense. Nothing seemed to go together.

"So, what do you think this is all about?" asked Ms. Daly. "Respond one at a time please."

I made my best educated guess. "To create a first-aid kit?"

"To make mummies," called out Steven from the back.

"Exactly," said Birdie. "But green ones."

"I like your ideas," said Ms. Daly. "But you people are as wrong as snow in July in Michigan." We laughed as she glanced out the window as snow flurries drifted down from the heavy gray sky. We were all buzzing with excitement since our first snowfall came early this year. "Now I'll give you one last clue." Ms. Daly poured a quarter cup of water and mixed it with the powder to make a bright green liquid. Then, in one huge swallow, she drank it.

I gasped. In chemistry, you never ever *ever* drink experiments. Mostly because chemicals can be way too hot or cold, or even worse, toxic.

Ms. Daly waggled a finger. "All right, kiddos. Don't do this at home. Or ever. I only drank that because I knew what it was." She pulled out a packet of lime-flavored drink mix. "See?"

"Yum!" Memito bopped in his seat. "Smells like lime and watermelon and summer. I'm drinking a gallon!"

"Sorry. Not today," said Ms. Daly. "This afternoon, we're making fake tattoos."

A bunch of kids cheered, especially Birdie, who's an amazing artist. "I already know what tattoo I'm going to make," she said with a shy smile. Of course she did. Back in kindergarten, when I was drawing stick figures, she was figuring out shading. Now, in fifth grade, I'm still drawing stick figures and she's making *Mona Lisa*s.

"Great!" I said to Birdie. "I mean about knowing what you're going to do for your tattoo." Only I was glad she didn't ask me what I planned to do. Because I seriously had no idea. When it comes to art, my brain definitely flash freezes.

Birdie studied me. "Just draw what you like."

"Oh sure, that would be real easy."

I like rockhopper penguins, but I don't think I could draw one.

And I *love* chemistry, but how would I draw that? Chemistry is the part of science that deals with the form of matter and its surroundings. Like how a snowflake sparkles on your winter jacket, how cheese gets gooey on your pizza, and why there are shimmering pink rings around Saturn. So yeah, pretty much everything.

I had to find one awesome tattoo idea. But what?

From the box, Ms. Daly pulled out more drink mix packages, like blueberry, strawberry, grape, lemon, cherry, and watermelon. "You're going to pick one of these. If you're adventurous, you can pick a bunch. Each color requires a quarter cup of cornstarch and a quarter cup of warm water. Mix up your ingredients, and you're just about ready to make your tattoos."

Soon enough, all the chemistry club members raced up to grab materials, and Ms. Daly handed out the directions on how to make fake tattoos.

I chose watermelon since pink is my favorite color. Birdie choose grape, lime, and orange. Back at our table, after studying the directions, we got started. Only when I dipped my cotton swab into the pink mixture and tested it, it dribbled down my arm.

Meanwhile Birdie had already painted the outline of a parrot on her skin. "That's so good," I said. "Not just good. *Amazing*."

Her amazingness made me feel a little bit like giving up. Or maybe trying something easy like a smiley face.

Birdie studied the streaky drips on my arm. "Did you put in too much water?"

"Probably." Grabbing the spoon, I spun the mixture so hard it swirled like a whirlpool.

Birdie blew on the parrot tattoo on her arm. "See how it's lightening up? That means I can use the liquid bandage to lock it into place. Then I'll get started on a new color. Orange for the tail feathers."

"That will look great, Birdie. Guess I'll make a smiley face."

"Mmmhhm." But she wasn't really listening. She was stirring up the orange.

I smushed my swab down in the beaker. Maybe that would get the pink mixture to stick to the tip of the swab.

Then, out of the corner of my eye, I spotted something incredible across the room. Something incredible and way unexpected!

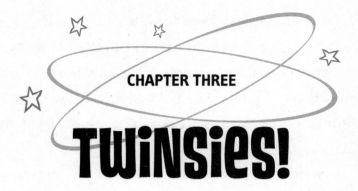

CHAPTER THREE

TWINSIES!

Statistical significance (noun). When the result of an experiment doesn't happen randomly. For example, every time you leave a crayon on the back seat of your parents' van on a hot day, it will melt. You might decide that, maybe just maybe, it's a much better idea to draw with your crayons instead!

THE NEW GIRL, TALA, WAS PAINTING a purple atom on her arm. She had everything right. A nucleus, the densely packed center, and zippy electrons all around it.

I bolted out of my seat and stood next to her. "Hi, I'm Kate Crawford. Sorry I didn't introduce myself before. I love *love* your tattoo!"

"Thanks. It combines two of my favorite things. The color purple and space."

"I thought that"—I pointed to the three intersecting

ovals above her wrist—"was an atom."

"It is." She put down her cotton swab and laughed. "Almost all of an atom is empty space. And that's no different than out there." She pointed up. "Outer space is mostly empty except for particles that are super far apart. Plus dust. And a few other things."

I studied Tala's atom. It was such an important concept in chemistry. The building block of the whole universe. I could practically feel the molecules in my body vibrating with excitement. Why hadn't I thought of making an atom?

"Hey, Birdie," I called out, motioning with my arm. "You've got to see this." But she didn't answer. With her head bent down, she focused on her parrot tattoo. It was going to be a masterpiece. When Birdie does her art, the whole world pretty much goes away.

"I can make you an atom, too." Tala dipped her cotton swab back into the purple mixture.

"Really? That would be amazing!" Grabbing an alcohol pad out of my pocket, I wiped down my forearm, and blew on it. "I'm ready."

As Tala painted on my atom, I asked her a bunch of questions. And soon, even though we had just met, it felt

like we had known each other way longer. Tala was easy
to talk to. She told me that her mom was a family doctor
and that they had moved to Michigan from California
because she had joined a new medical practice. And that
her new place was way bigger. Back in San Jose, her family had lived in a cramped two-bedroom
apartment.

"Here we have a whole house."
She stuck her arms out wide. "Talk
about space. Wow. My little sister
and I don't have to share a room.
Which is good since she's a total
slob. I can hang up all of my
NASA posters. When I grow up,
I want to become an astronaut."

"That's so cool. I want to be a
chemist," I said.

"Maybe we can work on the International Space
Station together. And stare down at our big, blue marble
spinning through the galaxy."

"Our marble?" I asked, confused.

"Oh, the blue marble is kind of like a nickname for
Earth," said Tala. "It's from a famous photograph taken

by the crew of Apollo 17, which was the last moon landing, a long time ago in 1972."

"Wow. You know so much about space," I said, and she beamed. I told her that her International Space Station idea sounded like an awesome plan. Then we started talking more about science and astronomy. Tala really knew so many cool facts. Like how comets are sometimes called dirty snowballs.

"I bet you didn't have that back in California." I pointed to the actual snow outside.

"Nope. Not unless you drove hours up to the mountains. Seeing snow in my neighborhood is the best thing ever. I just hope it sticks around so I can take lots more photos today. I want to send them to my friends back home." She paused. "My old home. This is home now." I thought I heard a sigh, but maybe I was imagining things.

Then she told me about the science club she'd belonged to at her old school. Last year, they celebrated the start of winter break by setting off rockets that zoomed above the houses.

"That's so cool!" I glanced at the purple atom above my wrist. "Hey, we match." We put our wrists together, shook hands, and laughed.

"Twinsies," said Tala.

"Yes, twinsies!" Her old club got me thinking about rockets. "My little brother, Liam, loves everything to do with outer space. It would be great to learn how to make a rocket to show him. Plus, it would just be so cool."

"I definitely could show you."

"Really? Seriously? Wow. His birthday party is coming up, and he'd love it."

"Sure. I could even come over and help you make the rockets for the party."

"Yes!" And then we tapped our new tattoos together and giggled at our new secret handshake. More than anything, I wanted to make Liam's birthday party extra special. Last year, when he had turned five, it hadn't worked out so well. A week before his party, I had gotten a little stomach bug. I was better pretty fast, but then the morning of Liam's party, he said his tummy felt like there was a fish flopping inside of it. A few minutes later, he threw up all over his lion paper plates right before the guests were supposed to arrive. Mom had to frantically text all the parents and cancel the party. It was so sad since we had spent hours decorating the house in a lion theme with papier-mâché lions and a fake den where the kids would hide. Liam wore a lion tail and ears.

Even though it wasn't my fault, I felt responsible for the party being canceled. After all, I was the one who had gotten Liam sick and ruined everything. That very day, I had promised myself I would make it up to him. That for this next birthday, when he turned six, I would use all of my science skills to make his party awesome. A few weeks ago, when he said he wanted a space-themed party, I was all in.

"Seriously, I can't tell you what good timing this is," I told Tala as she continued to work on putting another atom on her upper arm, "since my brother's party is coming up in two weeks. Meeting you feels like it's . . ." I almost said *magical*. But I don't believe in magic. "Statistically significant." That basically means a result that's not due to chance.

"Well, maybe we could also make rockets here?" Tala put down her cotton swab. "Like a special club project or something?"

"That would be great," I said. "I'm going to ask Ms. Daly and see what she thinks."

"Awesome." Tala waved her tattooed arm.

Later, I tried to ask Ms. Daly about the rocket. I really

did, but every time I went up to her, she was busy helping out kids who were asking for stuff like more drink
mix packages for their tattoos.

Finally, at the end of our meeting, I hurried over to
where Ms. Daly was wiping down the counter. "I wanted
to talk about a new project idea," I said. "Launching
rockets!"

Ms. Daly ran her fingers through her short hair as
if my suggestion made her head itch. "If the rockets
involve actual fuel and the potential for anything explosive, my answer is going to be no. I don't need to tell
you I'm retired air force, do I? That safety is number one
and—"

"Well, I'm not sure if the rockets use fuel. I mean, I
don't know the details, but I'll find out.
And do research!" Then I nodded over
at the table, where Tala was working
on her third atom tattoo. I explained
how Tala had launched rockets at her
old school.

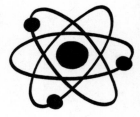

"Here's a suggestion, Kate." Ms. Daly glanced up at
the clock. It was 3:45 p.m. "Get me when I'm not right
at cleanup and when it's not time to go. Show me that

the rockets are safe. Plus, give me a list of materials and a budget, and then, and only then, will I consider it."

"You got it!" After I was done with my research, Ms. Daly had to say yes! Just a couple of months ago, she had let me breathe fire after I had written a detailed report about it. Compared with that, launching rockets should be a breeze.

CHAPTER FOUR

A SPACE-FILLED DAY

Crystallography (noun). This is the kind of chemistry that studies the crystal structure of molecules that contain elements like gold and iron. In order to understand the crystals, scientists need to study the atoms. In order to understand our friends, wouldn't it be nice to have a crystal ball?

AFTER CHEMISTRY CLUB WAS OVER, Birdie and I walked home together. Normally, I get a ride with my mom. And Elijah comes too, along with Liam, who talks nonstop. But last week, my mom had promised Birdie and me that we could bike home together, as long as there wasn't ice on the ground and it wasn't snowing.

Well, obviously, with the flurries today, that plan

had been scrapped. But we had still decided we were up for a mile-long hike.

Although the snow was light, we wore boots, thick parkas, gloves, and wool caps.

The wind whipped snow flurries around us. "Snowflakes are ice crystals," I said.

"True." Birdie sounded like she was both bored and disappointed, which didn't make sense.

Tilting up my chin, I watched the snowflakes as they cascaded downward. "Amazing that each one is made up of water molecules. Two hydrogen atoms bond with one oxygen atom. Then they dance themselves to form six-sided rings. Hexagons." I stuck out my tongue. A snowflake landed right on the tip. "Hexagons taste good. But they could use a little sugar."

"Uh-huh," said Birdie.

"Or maple syrup."

"Sure," said Birdie.

Whipping around, I clapped my gloved hands together. "Oh, did I tell you? I asked Ms. Daly if we could launch rockets during chemistry club."

"Really?"

"Yeah. I just have to come up with a plan. But hopefully, she'll say yes." Then I excitedly told her about the rocket launch at Tala's old science club back in California. And how she was going to help me with the rockets for Liam's birthday party. "He's going to love it!" I looked up at the sky, as if maybe I could somehow catch sight of a twinkling star in the middle of the day. "Tala's an expert on outer space. She wants to be an astronaut. It's pretty awesome, right?"

"I guess."

"With Tala around, it feels like rockets are in the air. Get it? In the air?"

"Yeah. I get it." Birdie fiddled with her bracelet.

"Maybe we could use the leftover drink mix to make slushies. Rocket launching and slushies. Oh! And we could make cherry ones, your favorite."

Birdie shrugged. "Sounds all right. But it could be snowing." She pointed up at the milky sky. "Or sleeting. Doesn't really seem to be the best idea."

"Well, we won't know unless we try. Which is the point, right? Of doing experiments, I mean."

"Sure. Well, see you later." Birdie hiked up her

backpack and started to turn left onto Oak Lane Court.

"Wait. You don't need to go so soon. We could—" I dug my gloves into a bank of fresh snow. "Have a snowball fight. Or make snow angels!" Birdie loved tracing halos over our angels, which would make them look almost real.

"Not now."

"My dad bought that special hot chocolate mix. And we can put mini marshmallows in it."

Birdie shrugged. "I'm not in the mood."

"Is everything okay?"

"Fine."

"Are you sure?"

"I just want to go home," she said.

"Okay. Another time then!" As I trudged back alone to my house, I felt a little bit sad and disappointed. It was Friday. And Fridays mean the weekend. And weekends mean long playdates or sleepovers.

Then I wondered if Birdie wasn't feeling well. I should have asked her. I whipped around to see if she was still on the sidewalk, but she was already inside. Then I thought about something I could do that might cheer her up. Maybe Mom and I could bake chocolate chip cookies and drop them off at her house. Chocolate always makes Birdie feel better.

But my mom says that when someone is grumpy, sometimes you just need to give them space. So maybe I should let her be.

I guess it was just a space-filled day. And it was just about to get even space-ier. I'm not sure if that's a word, but it really should be. Which got me wondering more about actual outer space and how it wasn't really empty but had molecules spaced far apart. And that got me wondering about Tala. What would she be doing on a Friday? Probably something awesome like looking through a telescope at the stars in the sky.

CHAPTER FIVE

THE BAD LUCK KID

Improbability principle (noun). This is the idea in science that coincidences might not be rare. For example, if there is a classroom of thirty students, the chances that two kids will have the same birthday is really high! Which means a double birthday party at school!

THE MINUTE I FINISHED HANGING up my coat, Liam burst into the mudroom. "I'm bad luck," he moaned.

"What? You're the opposite of that. Who made the most goals on his soccer team?"

"Me."

"Who saw the giant green frog at the county fair?"

"Me."

"Who got to be Student of the Month in kindergarten?"

"Me. But Desmond said I'm the most unlucky kid ever." Desmond was Liam's best friend and he said lots of silly things. Like that he ate slugs for breakfast and had invisibility superpowers.

"C'mon." I plunked off my boots. "Let's talk in the kitchen."

"Desmond said that 'cause I'm born on December thirteenth, my whole life is bad luck. He said thirteen is a really unlucky number."

"That's just a superstition. And it's not true."

"Then how come I broke my collarbone when we went to Florida? And lost my Batman sneakers? Plus, the tooth fairy forgot to give me money last month."

"You got money, Liam."

"Yeah, but the day after I was supposed to. And last year, my birthday party didn't even—"

"Stop! Seriously. The thirteenth is an awesome day. All that stuff has nothing to do with the number thirteen. You should stop talking about it."

And if I was being honest, I just couldn't handle hearing about Liam's non-party last year. Even rescheduling it didn't work out, because of a snowstorm and then it was winter break. Plus, a bunch of Liam's friends all got sick, too. That's why Mom and Dad had promised Liam an extra-special birthday party this year.

Usually, he can only invite ten friends.

This year they said he could invite twenty. Basically, his entire kindergarten class. But right now, Liam wasn't focusing on the positive. He was as negative as an electron.

Liam pouted so that his bottom lip stuck out like a bulldog's. "Desmond said bad things will happen at my birthday party. Catastrophes."

"Ignore Desmond. He's trying to get your goat."

"I don't have a goat." Liam almost sort of smiled. "I have a dog." He pointed to where our rust-colored retriever, Dribble, lay in front of the back door.

" 'Getting your goat' is an expression. Desmond was trying to tease you. Let's talk about happy things—like your party decorations."

Liam's shoulders went less slumpy. "It's got to be everything outer space."

"I know, but let's decide on the details."

"Okay." His eyes sparkled and the world seemed

almost sunny, even though the snow was coming down faster outside.

I grabbed two packets of hot chocolate and a bag of miniature marshmallows. "I think we need a treat." I filled up our teakettle with water.

"If you're making hot chocolate, count me in," said Dad, strolling into the kitchen. He's a psychologist, which means he helps people with their problems and sometimes does his paperwork in his home office. "I'm ready for a break."

"On it." I whipped out another packet of hot chocolate.

"Katie's planning my birthday party," shouted Liam. He's the *only* person I let call me Katie. Although his cheeks were still red from being upset, a smile was on his face.

We plopped down at the kitchen table, and Dad grabbed a yellow pad from a drawer. "I'll be the note taker. I can't wait to hear your ideas," he said.

"Same here," I said.

"Same not here," said Liam with a giggle. "'Cause I'm in outer space!"

CHAPTER SIX

SEEING IS BELIEVING

Electron microscope (noun). This is a special microscope where beams of electrons allow us to see teeny-tiny things like molecules and even atoms. That means you couldn't look at anything big, like your pet snake. For one thing, it would be too wriggly!

AFTER I DUMPED THE CONTENTS of the cocoa packets in our mugs, we discussed the all-important party decorations. Like what kind of plates we needed and how we could have a rocket station. Then I came up with the idea of using some liquid nitrogen to create a Jupiter-like atmosphere right outside the garage. I bet Mom could borrow some liquid nitrogen from Ms. Daly, since she's the principal and all.

"Great idea, Kate, to have the station outside," said Dad, "since liquid nitrogen is freezing cold and can be dangerous."

"You could drop a vat of hot water into a bucket of the liquid nitrogen. Then poof! It would get all cloudy. And look just like Jupiter. Make sure to wear a lab coat, gloves, and goggles, though," I said.

"Yup, I got it." Dad made the okay sign. "Safety first. Remember what Dr. Caroline taught us."

Dad always reminds me about Dr. Caroline when he wants me to be extra careful. She's my favorite chemist on YouTube. And she visited our school for STEM Night last month, and I met her!

"Yay! We're going to Jupiter," screamed Liam, interrupting my thoughts about Dr. Caroline's visit. He then said instead of party hats, he wanted everyone to wear alien antenna headbands.

"That's awesome, but aliens aren't real," I said.

"As far as we know," said Dad with a wink. "Just because you can't see something doesn't mean it doesn't exist. Once upon a time, people didn't know about molecules or atoms. Then scientists theorized they existed, and later we developed technology to see them. But even before the electron microscope was invented, atoms still existed."

"I guess that makes sense when it comes to aliens, but only sort of." I told them about how in chemistry club, the new girl, Tala, brought up how astronomers theorized black holes existed even though they couldn't see them. "Right now, we don't have evidence to really know if little green outer space people exist."

"But if we get evidence we could?" asked Liam.

"Exactly," said Dad.

Liam thumped his chest. "I'm gonna find some space monsters."

"Go for it," I said.

Whiiiiiiieeee.

A high-pitched screech came from the other side of the kitchen. I jumped out of my chair. "What's that?" I asked, jerking my head around.

"I think it's called the teakettle," said Dad.

"Oh, right." Liam and I both laughed. All the talk about bad luck and aliens had spooked me. Grabbing

the kettle, I filled the mugs with the hot water. "Let's just stick to science. Like planets, comets, stars, and—"

"Black holes that suck everything into them," said Liam with big eyes. "Hey, I want chocolate doughnut holes at my party. Oh, and black hole key chains as party favors."

Dad tapped his pen. "I can't write that fast—slow down."

"Cake!" yelled Liam. "With planets on it. And a spaceship. No. It should look like a planet or a moon." He held out his arms. "With giant craters."

Dad thought a minute. "How about a cheesecake? Everyone knows the moon is made out of green cheese."

"It's actually made from rock, and there's silicon and magnesium and iron in the middle," I said excitedly. "Tala was telling me about it. She loves space just like Liam."

"I don't want a cheesecake." Liam harrumphed.

"Have you ever had one?" asked Dad.

"No, and I'm not going to. Ever." Liam squinched up his face. "Cheesecake is yucky."

"What about cupcakes, then?" I said brightly.

Liam folded his arms. "I want an ice cream cake with a Saturn on it. 'Cause the rings look like a racetrack. And

I want Mr. Arvanites at McSweeny's to make it. Desmond got an ice cream cake there, and it looked like a real land of dinosaurs. With a T. rex on it. And grass that was icing." He licked his lips.

That's when Mom strode into the kitchen. "I couldn't help but overhear the last part of your conversation," she said, "and it's much more interesting than the budget meeting I just finished up at school." She placed her hand on Liam's shoulder. "Honey, you invited your entire class to come from eleven a.m. until two p.m. If we pick the ice cream cake up in the morning, it will melt before your guests arrive, and we don't have anyplace to store a large one."

"Sorry, buddy," said Dad, rubbing Liam's head.

Liam slumped in his chair. "It's not fair."

"Hey, I could pick up the cake in the wagon," I said. "It's only ten blocks away." Then I thought about how Birdie could come with me. As long as she was acting like herself again. Not all weird and distant. "I could get it during the party. Right before we eat," I added. "I could bring Birdie."

Dad took a sip of his hot chocolate. "I don't see why not."

"I guess as long as it's not snowing," said Mom.

"No. Let it snow, snow, snow!" Liam pointed out the window. "If it's a huge snowstorm, then my friends can stay with us an entire week!"

"Oh boy," said Mom. "If it's the snowstorm of the century, we'll have to take a rain check on the birthday party."

"Or rather a snow check." Dad handed Mom his mug of hot chocolate.

She took a slow sip. "All right. If your sister is careful, then yes, you can have your ice cream cake. And it would definitely be good to have Birdie with you."

"Yay!" Liam gave me a giant hug. "You're the best sister in the entire universe."

"Let's not forget the multiverse." Dad winked.

"I can't wait until my birthday," said Liam. "'Cause it's going to be the best luck day ever!"

"Definitely," I said, giving him a high five. "Because there is no such thing as bad luck. It's a scientific improbability."

"I sure hope so," said Liam, looking into his now empty mug.

"I know so," I said.

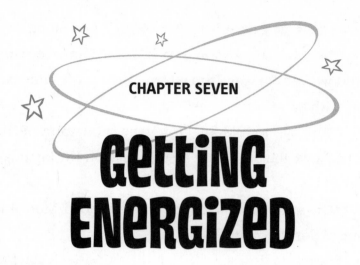

CHAPTER SEVEN

GEttiNG ENERGIZED

Fuel (noun). In scientific terms, fuels are molecules that have energy stored within their bonds, and can be found in pasta or cheesecake. Your body burns the molecules in food, and for many, fueling up is the best part of the day, especially if the fuel comes from dessert!

MONDAY MORNING HAD BEEN way too Monday-ish. Outside, it was gray, without a hint of sun or snow. In class, Birdie had been quiet, like she had caught the blahs. I wanted to do something to cheer her up but couldn't get her to crack a smile. It made me nervous.

During lunch, when Birdie and I sat down at our usual table, Memito and Elijah were already there, along with Avery and her best friend, Phoenix Altman.

"Anyone want to guess what's in this mystery meat?" asked Memito, pointing to his lunch tray.

"No thanks," said Phoenix, who's a vegetarian. She bit into her bean burrito.

"I don't care if it's a cooked shoe," said Elijah, stabbing his meat loaf. "I'm super hungry, so I'm going for the mystery meat."

"You're brave." I laughed. Birdie sort of smiled.

After a giant bite of my ham sandwich, I began to feel better. It was chemistry, of course. Once the sandwich arrived in my stomach, it plopped into a vat of acid, which converted my sandwich molecules into glucose—basically fuel. Yup, I could feel myself getting energized.

"Hey, isn't that the new girl?" said Avery. She nodded over at Tala, who was holding up a lunch bag, peering around at all of the tables as if she didn't quite know where to go.

"Hey, Tala, over here," I called out.

Leaning forward, Tala peered over at the drink station, looking a little confused.

Immediately, I popped out of my chair. Then I waved

my arms over my head like I was directing a plane at the airport. Tala was so cool, and I really wanted Birdie and the gang to get to know her better.

Smiling, Tala headed over to our table. "Sit here!" I patted my seat.

"Thanks." She set down a lunch bag. Today, her long wavy dark hair was pushed back in a bright yellow headband. Somehow, it made me think of the sun, which made me think of California, where she was from.

Plopping down in the empty seat on her other side, I said, "Welcome." Tala was sitting between me and Birdie. I quickly made introductions, because she was in Mrs. Que's fifth-grade class and we were all in Mrs. Eberlin's class.

Out of her lunch sack, Tala pulled a sandwich, an apple, a granola bar, and a small plastic container with the most delicious-smelling rice in it.

"Yum, what's that?" asked Memito.

"Garlic rice," said Tala, "leftovers from dinner. It's my lola's recipe."

"I want to meet your lola," said Memito. "What's a *lola*?"

Tala laughed. "She's my dad's mom. And you'd have

to fly to the Philippines, but sure." Tala grinned, and I couldn't help grinning, too.

"I'm so excited you're here," I said to Tala.

"Thanks," she replied.

"Seriously. I've been thinking about what you 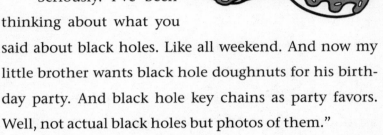 said about black holes. Like all weekend. And now my little brother wants black hole doughnuts for his birthday party. And black hole key chains as party favors. Well, not actual black holes but photos of them."

Meanwhile Birdie closed up her lunch bag, even though she had hardly eaten. She's honestly the slowest eater on the planet. But she usually finishes up everything, even if it's just as the bell rings. "I forgot something I have to finish in the art room," she murmured.

"Okay," I said, smiling a bit. But honestly, I felt disappointed that Birdie wasn't getting a chance to talk with Tala. I glanced up at the clock. "You've got seventeen minutes. I hope that's enough time."

"Yeah." Birdie stuffed her lunch bag into her backpack.

"Good luck!" called out Tala.

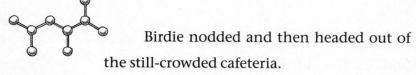 Birdie nodded and then headed out of the still-crowded cafeteria.

"When it comes to art, Birdie doesn't need luck," I explained to Tala. "She's super talented. Even something she sketches for two minutes looks better than anything I work on for hours. I'm even bad at stick figures."

"Me too," said Tala.

"I can't even draw a straight line unless I use a ruler. And even then, I mess up."

Tala laughed. For someone into serious stuff like astronomy, I could tell she knew how to have fun. Birdie, for one, needed to have some more fun right now. The rocket launch could be just the answer.

I turned to Tala. "Hey, I'm going to talk to Ms. Daly about the rocket launch idea tomorrow," I said. "She's in school all day on Tuesdays to work with the lower grades on science, and I've been thinking about it all weekend."

"That's great," said Tala, "because it sounds like the rockets—"

"Did someone say 'rockets'?" asked Elijah.

"Yup," I said.

Then Tala explained how she did a rocket launch with her old science club.

"Rockets use so much fuel," said Phoenix. "Although I've read that they have reusable rockets now!"

"These aren't real rockets," I said.

"Rockets made from soda bottles," explained Tala. "Baking soda, vinegar, and other stuff. Plus, for real height, you need to make a launchpad."

"Like how high will the rocket go? Your knee?" joked Elijah, pointing to his leg.

Tala threw up her arms. "Way, way high. Two stories, for sure."

"Whoa!" said Memito, gazing up at the ceiling.

"That's cool," gushed Avery. "One time at my dads' theater, we were doing a show about the Apollo moon landing, and instead of building model rockets, the set designer projected videos of them blasting off onto a backdrop."

"Actually, there's a secret to making the rockets really blast off," said Tala, "which is—"

"Shhhh." I put my finger to my lips. "Don't tell them. They'll have to work on their rockets to find out."

"Oh, I'll figure it out." Elijah thumped the table like a drum.

"Me too," said Memito.

"We'll see about that." I turned to Tala. "I think Ms. Daly will say yes to the rocket launch. But it's always better if you can give her as many reasons as possible. She likes to know the science behind stuff. And to make sure it's all safe. Do you want to come over after school so we can work on the plan? And the rockets for the party?"

"Definitely," she said. "That sounds like a blast!"

"A rocket blast, that is," I said, giggling at my own joke.

CHAPTER EIGHT

THE RIGHT STUFF

Baking soda (noun). A substance that reacts with acids (like vinegar) to form carbon dioxide gas. The scientific name for baking soda is sodium bicarbonate ($NaHCO_3$), and when you bake with it, it makes your cookies all soft and fluffy. Science sure can taste good!

"WELL, I THINK WE SHOULD do two kinds of rockets," said Tala. After school, we had planted ourselves at the kitchen table. Right away I had given her a tour of our house, and she had met Liam. Steaming mugs of hot chocolate sat in front of us.

"For Liam's party, you could make double balloon rockets," continued Tala. "And for the chemistry club, I think we should stick to baking soda bottle rockets."

After she explained the difference between the two, I told her it sounded like an awesome idea. For the balloon rockets, you needed long balloons like the kind for balloon animals and a few other supplies. And she said that when it was done, the rockets would whoosh all over the living room.

Dribble stood next to me, sniffing the hot chocolate, his brown eyes hopeful he would get some. I petted him behind his ears. "None for you, buddy. Bet you can't wait for the balloon rockets. You'll chase them all over, barking like mad. Of course, Liam's friends will love it." As if he could understand, Dribble thumped his tail.

I glanced at Tala as she blew on her hot chocolate. "Hey, will you tell me the secret ingredient for the baking soda bottle rocket?"

She tapped her chin. "Hmm. You like figuring out things, right?"

"Oh, yeah!"

With a sly smile, she nodded. "So you'll have to figure out the secret yourself."

"Well, I just solved a mystery," I said. "Last month Ms. Daly came up with an escape room. We were locked in a lounge at school and couldn't get out until we found an image of a deadly virus before this bad guy did. Even though it was nerve-racking, we were able to

solve all the puzzles. It was awesome!"

Tala took a sip of her hot chocolate. "Wow. I'm bummed I missed that. But it sounds like you'll have no problem learning the secret ingredient for the bottle rocket."

"I like the way you think," I said. Then I explained how I was planning on telling Ms. Daly how safe and fun the chemistry club rockets would be. Plus, Ms. Daly had access to almost all the supplies in her lab. It was important to let her know that our plan would be simple-ish, fun, and require materials that would be easy to access.

"I like the way you think, too," said Tala.

I grabbed one of Dad's yellow notepads. "I guess we can get started."

Tala wrote out a list of the items we would need for Liam's balloon rockets. And then a list of materials to make the rockets for chemistry club, including empty soda bottles, vinegar, baking soda, a cork, and a rocket base. Then, with a big grin on her face, she drew a giant X for the secret material.

"Is it a stopwatch?" I asked. "To see how long it takes for the rocket to explode?"

"Well, it's always good to time stuff. But no."

"A test tube?" I asked.

"No."

"Orange soda?" I asked.

"Nope."

"Paint? A dime? A wire?"

"No. No. No." She giggled.

"All right. I'm going to have to think about this. Let's move on to the balloon rockets for Liam's party."

"I heard my name!" screeched Liam as he sped into the kitchen. Then he eyed our steaming ceramic mugs. "Hey! You got hot chocolate. No fair."

I gestured at a lion-head-shaped mug across from me. It was a present from Grandpa Jack for Liam's birthday last year. I swallowed hard, remembering how sad Liam had been when his party was canceled. "Who do you think that mug is for?" I asked.

"An imaginary friend?" guessed Liam.

"You, silly!" I shook my head.

He picked up the mug of hot chocolate and blew on it. "Thanks, Kate. It's got marshy mellows."

"Marshmallows," I corrected with a wink.

"Look, Liam," said Tala. "Here's a list of materials

you'll need for the double balloon rockets for your birthday party."

"Cool!" shouted Liam.

She read out the list: "Balloons, straws, light clamps, fishing line, cardboard rolls, clear tape, a balloon pump, scissors."

I clapped my hands. "Yay! We've pretty much got everything. Dad has tons of fishing line." Jumping up, I paced around the table. "The cardboard rolls sound perfect for the rocket body."

Tala sipped her hot chocolate. "Yup, since it's got to be aerodynamic."

"What does that mean?" asked Liam, who plopped down in a seat across from Tala.

"Well, aerodynamics is the study of forces and how easily an object goes through the air," said Tala.

"Pretty easy!" Liam picked up a gooey marshmallow out of his mug and tossed it into his mouth. "Like this!"

"Exactly," I said with a snort. "Between the two of you, it's like I've entered the astronaut zone. Right now, I feel like my life is out of this world." I covered my mouth. "Wow. I've turned into Ms. Daly. Sorry about that. I can't stop making corny jokes."

"I forgive you," said Tala.

"I don't." Liam crossed his arms. "Space isn't funny. It's serious. 'Cause it's for my party. And it's going to be the awesomest with the yummiest ice cream cake. Even better than Desmond's dinosaur one."

"We know," I said.

A few minutes later, Tala and I got started getting the supplies ready for Liam's double rockets. We figured we'd decorate the toilet paper rolls so they would look extra cool. Luckily, in our house we always save rolls for art supplies.

I dragged out tempera paint so we could paint the rolls sky blue. While I laid down newspaper on the table, Tala grabbed brushes, and Liam waited with his smock on. All of the art supplies made me think of my best friend. I felt a weird tightness in my throat like I was getting a cold. But it wasn't a cold.

"I wish Birdie was here," I admitted. "She'd know how to mix the blue and white to make the perfect color."

"Yeah, judging from that tattoo she made, she's an incredible artist," said Tala.

At first Birdie had said she was going to come over after school, but then she backed out at the last minute because she had to help her sister. She wouldn't tell me what they had to do though. Honestly, I was starting to get kind of worried. But if something was really wrong, Birdie would have told me. We always tell each other everything. Just a couple of weeks ago, Birdie had confessed that she borrowed her mom's new headphones without asking.

And I admitted that while shopping I had dropped my gum and could only get 90 percent of it off the mall floor.

So yeah, we always tell each other everything.

"Too bad Birdie couldn't be here," said Tala.

"Yeah, well, she told me that something came up." I shrugged and tried not to let it bother me.

"I wish I were better when it comes to art like Birdie," said Tala.

"But you made that atom tattoo that was so cool." Mine had washed off over the weekend but it had been pretty awesome.

"That's all I can do. Atoms. Stars. Suns. And bunny rabbits."

"That's more than me." I laughed, holding up a paintbrush. "I only trust myself to make smiley faces and stars."

After some experimenting, we managed to mix

49

together a sky blue that looked pretty good. Then we painted all the tubes and laid everything out to dry.

"This is boring," moaned Liam. "It's taking forever."

"Well, you're not supposed to stare at it. It's like watching water boil," I said. "Time slows down when you do that."

"Actually, that's not true. Strong gravity slows space-time," said Tala.

"Whoa," said Liam. "That sounds cool." Then he stuck his finger on one of the paint-covered toilet paper rolls. "Still wet," he said.

After convincing him that it would be much better to go outside and play fetch with Dribble because the back patio was clear of snow, he trudged off to put on his jacket and boots.

"Liam's not exactly Mr. Patient. But neither am I," I admitted. "I can't wait to show Ms. Daly why your rocket launch is a good idea."

Then we thought of the perfect spot for rockets: the field outside of the school. We made a plan to get to school early the next day and ask Ms. Daly to make a decision about the launch.

She just had to say yes!

CHAPTER NINE

THE PROPOSAL

Proposal (noun). This is a paper that proposes a research project in science, and scientists hope that the proposal will help them get money to fund the project. You could write up a proposal to clean your neighborhood pond, so you can get funding to buy nets and trash bags to make the job easier!

ONCE TALA LEFT, I turned our ideas into a proposal. Scientists write proposals to get grants, which give them money to do their project.

I wanted to make the proposal official, so I typed it up and put it into an orange folder.

The next morning, Tala and I met up in front of the school. We were early, twenty minutes before the first bell rang.

"Ms. Daly is big on being on time, from her air force

days," I explained to Tala, who had dressed up for the occasion. As we walked into the school, I admired her sweater with silver ribbons woven through it, and she had silver ribbons in her hair, too. In my jeans and sweatshirt, I felt a little plain. "So anyway," I continued. "Ms. Daly even taught us military time. Scientists use it, too. They have a twenty-four-hour clock to avoid errors and confusion. So one thirty p.m. is really thirteen thirty hours."

"Cool," said Tala. "I know astronauts use a twenty-four-hour clock, but I didn't know other scientists did, too." She blew on her bangs as we stood outside the science lab. "I'm kind of nervous," she admitted.

I waved the folder. "Nothing to worry about. We have our proposal. She'll love it." I glanced at the door and knocked.

Nobody answered. It was open though, so Tala and I walked in. Ms. Daly stood near the sink frowning at the tile floor.

"Um, hi, Ms. Daly," I said. "Is everything okay?"

She grabbed a rag off the table. "It's not coming up." She pointed at the floor, which was shiny-looking in one spot. "And it's sticky as flypaper."

"What happened?" asked Tala.

"I thought it was just water. But now I'm pretty sure one of the fourth graders spilled some liquid adhesive bandage during chemistry club. Because it's not coming up. Earlier, I even tried soap."

"Wait! I've got an idea. What about acetone?" I exclaimed.

"You might be right, Kate. Go grab it."

I sped to the supply cabinet and pulled out a plastic bottle from the bottom shelf. I held it up. "Acetone will dissolve the glue because it's a solvent."

I handed Ms. Daly the bottle. "Here you go," I said.

"Thanks! Let's see." After throwing on some gloves, she poured the liquid onto the rag and rubbed the floor. Suddenly a smile stretched across her face. "This was the perfect idea, Kate."

I clapped my hands. "Yay for solvents!" Glancing at Tala, I grabbed my folder. "So we figured out what we need for our rocket launch," I said, pulling out the proposal.

Ms. Daly took a moment to read it. She was nodding, which was a good sign.

I pointed to the list of materials. "The budget will be low since we can ask students to bring in empty plastic bottles. And no flammables needed. Just a couple of chemical reactions that use some vinegar and baking soda, which we already have in the lab. The rockets will go super high because of a special material that Tala won't tell me about. She says I have to figure it out."

Beside me, Tala nodded.

"Well, you can tell me," said Ms. Daly.

Tala leaned forward and whispered in her ear.

"Aha!" said Ms. Daly. "That makes a lot of sense because of all the pressure."

"Oh, you've given me a clue," I said. "Now I'll figure it out."

"I'm sure you will, Kate." Ms. Daly winked at me. "I believe in that brain of yours."

"So does this mean the chemistry club gets to have a rocket launch too?" I asked.

"Yes," said Ms. Daly. "And I think doing it the

weekend before winter break is a great idea. That way, we can have the field to ourselves on Saturday, which would be good for safety." She whipped out her phone. "And the weather appears as if it will cooperate." She smiled. "Not that weather forecasts are perfect. But they are based on science."

Later, out in the hall, Tala started making some cool moves. She twisted around, kicked out her legs, and twirled three times with a clap and a snap. Elijah and Birdie both watched.

"What's that called?" I asked.

"My happy dance," said Tala. And I laughed because it made me happy just watching her. "Want to learn how?" she asked.

"Oh yeah!" I shouted.

I turned to Birdie and Elijah. "Want to learn with me?"

Elijah shrugged. "Sure, why not?"

Birdie squished up her face, like my question was a bitter lemon. "No thanks."

"But you love dancing," I said, confused and a little frustrated.

Birdie shook her head, which made no sense. Just

a few months ago, we had learned the steps of an old dance from YouTube. It was called the pretzel, and we had gotten as tangled up together as a game of Twister. We had laughed so hard that we had cried.

Right now, I almost felt like crying. But I held in any tears. This was supposed to be a happy moment. We were going to have a rocket launch.

"All you have to do is twist around, kick out your legs twice, then spin, spin, spin with a clap and a snap," said Tala, demonstrating the moves. "Now it's your turn."

There was no way this moment was going to be spoiled. I twisted, kicked, twirled, clapped, and snapped. Then wow, did I get dizzy.

"Glad you're not on the dance team," said Birdie, which seemed a little mean and not like her at all. I wanted to say something back to her, but I didn't want to get into a fight.

"That was good, Kate," said Tala. "Except it looked like you were trying to kick a soccer ball into a goal."

"Yeah. I was worried you thought my head was a soccer ball," joked Elijah.

Birdie let out a low chuckle. Okay, maybe I was imagining all of this drama, which wasn't there.

"Hey, I'm going next," said Elijah, who immediately got the happy dance perfect, except for the end when he snapped instead of clapped.

I glanced over at Birdie. Although her lips tugged into a tiny smile, her eyes weren't smiling at all. Then I thought about something. My dad always says when something doesn't feel right, just ask general questions.

I studied my best friend. "What's wrong?"

"If you can't figure it out, I'm not going to tell you." Then Birdie darted away down the hall.

I stared in her direction for a while before I heard Tala whisper, "I don't think Birdie likes me."

I whipped around and looked at Tala, confused. "No way," I said. "You're awesome. How could Birdie not like you?"

CHAPTER TEN

LOOKING FOR ANSWERS

Critical point (noun). The moment when you can't tell the difference between two phases, like a liquid and a gas. For example, when water is at a really high pressure and temperature (like 800°F), water and steam look the exact same. How crazy is that?!

BY FRIDAY I STILL HADN'T FIGURED OUT what was up with Birdie. We still talked, sat next to each other in the beanbag chairs during free read, and ate lunch together, but it didn't feel right. She was too quiet. I had to start our conversations. Sometimes during recess, which was outside this week since it wasn't too snowy, Birdie would just stay in the classroom and draw in her sketchbook.

But now after school at chemistry club, we were all excited to begin working on our rockets, since we had been collecting materials for them all week. By the front counter, Elijah, Memito, and Jeremy Rowe were using stencils to put their rocket names onto the tube part of their rockets (Pewter Scooter, Thunder Kiss, Mad Missile 13). Julia Yoon and Skyler Rumsky were cutting out fins. Avery, Phoenix, and Tala were making nose cones with a bunch of fourth graders. Ms. Daly scurried around the back of the lab, organizing supplies.

With a hot glue gun, I was about to stick on a piece of paper over my plastic bottle. "Light blue's nice, right?" I asked Birdie.

"I don't know," she said. "It might blend into the sky." Birdie shrugged. "It'd make the rocket hard to see."

I pulled out a violet sheet of paper. "How about this? Mighty Purple Force—activate!" Birdie just sort of shrugged again. She didn't giggle like she usually did when I brought up our old make-believe game. When we were in kindergarten, we used to pretend we were super-heroes with purple capes and elemental control, which was a fancy way of saying we could control the weather.

"Now with my powers, I can make sure it's going to

59

be warm and sunshiny." I nodded over at Tala, who was showing Phoenix and Avery how to roll their nose cones for their rockets. "Like in California."

"Sure," said Birdie. "That would be nice." But she didn't sound convinced. She didn't sound like she thought anything was nice. Suddenly, I wanted some answers. I had to ask the one question that had started to grow bigger and bigger in my mind like a weed that wanted to overtake all of my other regular thoughts.

"Is it because you think Tala doesn't like you?" I asked. "Because she does. She said your art was amazing."

"Sure."

"No, really. She went on and on."

Birdie didn't look up at me. She studied the silver sequins on the body of her rocket.

"The only reason she's across the room with Phoenix and Avery right now is because she thinks you don't like her." I inspected the now purple middle section of my bottle rocket.

"I don't know Tala," said Birdie. "So how can I not like her?"

"True, but you could get to know her." I stepped closer to Birdie and lowered my voice. "Could you tell me what is really going on? Honestly, I'm trying to guess what's wrong, but I'm getting kind of tired of it. It's like trying to detect that moment when ice melts and becomes water. You just can't quite see it."

"You're getting tired of guessing?" she squeaked.

"A little. Maybe. Yeah." This whole conversation was making me uneasy. Maybe because we were in the middle of the lab with others around. I studied the flecks in the tiles on the floor. I glanced around the room. And then I spotted Memito and Elijah arguing about something, and I realized exactly what I needed to do.

CHAPTER ELEVEN

SOMETHING TO DO WITH PRESSURE

Boyle's law (proper noun). This law says that the pressure of a gas goes up as the volume of its container gets smaller. Just like if you squeeze one part of the balloon (like a dog leg or monkey tail), the size of the balloon decreases and the pressure increases. If you squeeze the dog leg really hard, the pressure will increase so much that the balloon will explode! *POP!*

OVER BY THE SUPPLY TABLE, Elijah and Memito were arguing about the secret material that would make our rockets really soar. And I realized I hadn't figured it out yet either. All I knew is that it had something to do with pressure. And right now, honestly, I was feeling a lot of that.

"Oh, I have to do something!" I said to Birdie, who

glanced back at me with a confused expression. Heading to the middle of the lab, I explained, "I've got to make an educated guess."

I stopped in front of the supply table.

"If all the supplies are here, one of them should be the special material," I said, looking over at Tala for confirmation.

"You're right." Tala gave a thumbs-up. "It's definitely right here."

Jeremy flipped a coin into the air. The streak of purple in his blond hair flopped in his eyes. "I bet which one of you would get it right." He pointed at Memito and Elijah and then me. "I said you, Kate."

"You shouldn't bet." I shook my head, but privately I felt a little happy about it. And surprised, since some-times in the past, Jeremy wanted me to lose, whether it was a pickup game of soccer or the science fair.

Memito scooped up a plastic water bottle. "How about this?"

Tala shook her head. "It's essential but not a secret way to make the best rocket ever."

"The nose cone? Right? That's it?" asked Elijah.

"Nope," said Tala.

"How about the sequins?" piped up Birdie, who was standing a bit farther away from the table than the rest of us. My heart gave a little squeeze of happiness. She sounded almost like her regular self.

"Sequins are just decoration," said Tala.

"Decoration is essential." I nodded at Birdie's nose cone with its glittery swirls.

"Exactly. I mean, can you imagine going to a play without a set or curtains or costumes?" said Avery. "It would be so humdrum," she over-enunciated as if she were onstage.

"What do you think, Kate?" asked Jeremy. "I mean about the special material?"

My eyes swept over the materials. The heaps of bottles, colored paper, corks, little sequins, ribbons, and glitter for decoration.

"I think it's the cork," I said. "Because it seals the bottle to build up pressure, which produces the thrust."

"Good science," said Tala. "But still, no."

That's when Jeremy walked to the table, picked up a roll of toilet paper, and wrapped some around his neck.

"I have no clue what it is," he said. "But look at me; I'm a mummy!"

"Actually, he's much more than a mummy," said Tala. "Jeremy has the answer."

CHAPTER TWELVE

GETTING LAUNCHED

Endothermic reaction (noun). This is a chemical process that absorbs heat. When you mix vinegar and baking soda together, you have an endothermic reaction. This is because it takes a bunch of energy to break up the baking soda and vinegar molecules. It's sort of like how it takes more energy to pull apart stacked LEGOs than to collect them from two separate piles.

"ROLLS OF TOILET PAPER?" said Jeremy, his eyebrows raised in surprise. "That's the special material? Man, I should have bet on myself."

"Who would have thought toilet paper makes the rockets really fly?" I fished out another roll from a package under the supply table.

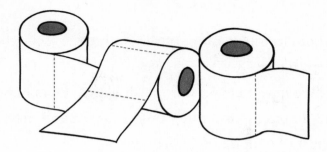

"TP is essential," said Jeremy, who balanced the roll on his head. "Especially because the rolls make nice hats."

"Ha ha," I said.

"The toilet paper is for little fuel packets of baking soda," said Tala, pulling off a sheet. "You put a table-spoon of baking soda in the middle of one square. Then cut off a piece of string and tie the corners of the toilet paper up into a mini package."

Phoenix strolled over. "It looks like a little sack of flour for dolls. So cute." I glanced over at Birdie, who was busy decorating her rocket with perfect stars.

"So they're fuel packets," I said. "The baking soda mixes with the vinegar to form a chemical reaction that changes the internal pressure to make the rocket go up into the sky."

"Exactly," said Tala. "You got it!" She did her happy dance. The twist, kick, twirls, then claps and snaps.

I did it, too. Because I really wanted to feel upbeat. "Happy dance!" we both cried.

"We have to make our rocket launch extra happy," I said, hoping that Birdie would hear me and maybe it might start to nudge a smile out of her.

Memito tossed up his rocket and caught it. "If you want it to be fun, you're going to need snacks."

"I was thinking we could make snow slushies," I said.

"Too cold." Grimacing, Memito shook his head. "I was thinking more like going to Brewster's Coffee Shop. They have Bunsen burners where you can roast marshmallows and make s'mores." He licked his lips. "Melted chocolate, marshmallow, and graham crackers. I'm getting hungry just thinking about it. Do you think Ms. Daly will let us go there after the rocket launch?"

"Maybe," I said.

"Will you ask?" Memito put his hands together.

"It's your idea," I said. "You should get credit."

"I don't care about credit. I just want to go to Brewster's. And she's more likely to say yes if you ask. Please," he said.

"Yeah, Kate," said Jeremy. "You know how much Ms. Daly looooooves you."

I shot him a look. Then I proceeded to march toward Ms. Daly, who was still in the back of the lab going through our supplies. As I walked on the tile floor, Memito cried, "Kate, stop!"

"What did I do?" I asked.

"You were about to step on a crack. Which would, you know, break your mother's back. And your mom is the principal."

I whipped around and stared at him. "You don't believe that, do you?"

"Pretty much. Sort of. Yeah. Anyway, the rocket launch is on the thirteenth, so I don't want to make it worse."

"What are you talking about?" I said, starting to panic. "We're having the rocket launch the weekend before winter break. Which is far away."

Glancing up from her clipboard, Ms. Daly said, "Actually, Kate, Saturday the thirteenth *is* the last Saturday before winter break. That's when we agreed to have the rocket launch."

My throat tightened. I guess I hadn't checked the calendar. The thirteenth was Liam's birthday party. At eleven a.m., just like the rocket launch!

"What am I going to do?" I shrieked. "That's the same time as my brother's birthday party!"

"I guess you can't do rockets with us," said Birdie.

No. That couldn't happen. I just had to figure out a way to do both!

CHAPTER THIRTEEN

THiNGS ARe GeTTING HeaVY

Mass (noun). This is a measurement of the quantity of matter, and it is not affected by your location. So your mass is the same on Earth and on Mars. Weight, on the other hand, measures how gravity acts upon the matter. So on Mars, you weigh much less than you do here on Earth!

"OKAY, EXPLAIN THIS TO ME ONE MORE TIME," said Mom. We stood in the dining room, me on one side of the table, Mom and Dad on the other. The only time we use the dining room is for Thanksgiving, Christmas, or when my grandparents visit from Texas. Or when we have serious family discussions, like right now.

"Because it seems to me, Kate," said Dad, "that you're overbooked."

"There is a two-letter word that's very helpful," said Mom. "*No*. Trust me. It will help you out in life if you learn how to say it when you're young."

"You guys don't get it," I said. "I can go to Liam's party and the chemistry club rocket launch."

"How?" asked Dad. "Are you going to ride a rocket ship at the speed of light to go back and forth?"

"Dad, first of all, people can't go the speed of light. If we tried, our mass would become infinite. So it's not possible, scientifically speaking."

"Okay, here's a plan that might work," said Mom. "You could clone yourself, Kate. As in make an exact copy."

"Well, sure. Maybe if I were a sheep." Scientists have successfully cloned sheep but not humans. I shook my head.

That's when Liam burst into the dining room. "Wait, Kate's turning into a sheep?"

"Ha ha, no," I said. Then just because I couldn't help it, I went *baaaa, baaaa*.

Liam *baaaaa*-ed back.

"Okay, that's it," said Mom. "I think I'm done."

"Terri, no," said Dad. "Give Kate a chance to actually explain her plan."

"So I'm going to be here at eleven," I said. "To welcome all the kids as the parents drop everyone off. Then I'll take the wagon to school. Set my rocket into the air," I said, "and then pick up the cake on my way back and—"

"You'll have Birdie with you," said Mom, "so you'll have company?"

"Well, um." I gazed at the floor. "Maybe. I'm not sure. We, uh, things have been weird between us lately."

"Have you spoken to her about it?" asked Dad.

"Sort of." I shrugged. "At school. But—"

"You need to have a real conversation with her," said Mom.

"That's a good idea," I said. "Once we actually talk, it will be better. The two of us can leave together from school, get the cake, and be back home to sing 'Happy Birthday.'"

"Yay! My ice cream cake!" cried Liam.

"And we can set off the double balloon rockets," I continued.

"Yay, double balloon rockets!" interrupted Liam again.

"Then Birdie and I will race back to be a part of the hot-chocolate-and-s'mores celebration at Brewster's," I finished.

"Well, I'm not so sure," said Mom. "It's a lot of going back and forth."

"I checked the weather forecast." I pointed to the family computer on the little desk by the kitchen. "It's supposed to be in the high forties. And no snow. Sun."

"Let her," begged Liam, clasping his hands. "Let her. Let her. Let her. She's already made awesome decorations. And fun stuff to do. Please! She wants to set off *rockets*. And she'll be back for the ice cream cake and the 'Happy Birthday' song and all the important parts."

At that moment, my love for Liam swelled. I mean, I always love my little brother, but right now it felt extra big.

"Well, I guess so," said Mom.

"I'll second that," said Dad.

"So that means yes," I said. "Because you know how much I want to be here for Liam. I mean, you know that, right? But Liam's party, honestly, wouldn't be as amazing

if it weren't for Tala. She's new and really cool. And doesn't really have a lot of friends yet. She and I planned both of these events together. And I just have to go to the chemistry club rocket launch so she's not alone."

"You don't need to convince us anymore," said Dad. "We already said yes."

"Just as long as you're back here on time to show everyone how to do the double balloon rockets and you pick up my cake," said Liam.

"Let's call to confirm the pickup time of the cake," said Mom. "It should be twelve thirty."

"Sounds good," I said.

Borrowing Dad's cell, I called Mr. Arvanites.

"Hello," he said curtly. "Who's this?" I explained that I was Kate Crawford, and I was calling to confirm the time of the cake pickup.

"The store's not open regular hours in the winter," he said. "So remember, I'm expecting you right at twelve thirty p.m."

"Don't worry," I said. "I won't be late." *Actually, we won't be late*, I thought. *Since I'm sure once I talk to Birdie, she'll be with me.* With my new plan in place, everything would work out. It had to. I also knew how much Tala wanted me to make the rocket launch. I couldn't wait to tell her the good news.

A few minutes later, I raced upstairs to my bedroom to call Tala. "So I can come," I said. "I worked it out."

"Phew," she said. "Because it wouldn't be the same without you. We planned it together," she said. "I'm so happy you'll be there."

"Me too," I said. "I definitely wouldn't want to miss it for anything."

CHAPTER FOURTEEN

LOOKiNG FOR a SOLUtiON

Soluble (adjective). If a scientist says that a substance is soluble, it means that it will dissolve. Lots of inks are soluble in alcohol, which means you can use it to wipe graffiti off desks and tables. But the best thing to do is not write on your desk in the first place!

"OKAY, LIAM," I SAID, "I think it won't fall down now." A little over a week had flown by, and I still had not been able to get to the bottom of what was going on with Birdie. It was Saturday, the morning of Liam's birthday, about an hour before the party. We were taping up a blanket of stars in the entryway to our house. It wasn't an actual blanket but a roll of paper with silver stars.

Liam studied the stars and all the other decorations. "They look good," he cried.

"I know!" And they did, especially with the helium-filled planet balloons floating in front. Saturn with its rings and Jupiter with its big spot looked especially cool. Earlier, we had tied them to strings so they wouldn't drift all the way up to the ceiling.

I peered down at my phone. Birdie still hadn't called me back. Earlier, I had tried to call her so that once we figured everything out, we could go to the rocket launch together and pick up Liam's cake. It was almost like she was avoiding me. In fact, all during school the past week, I had tried to get her alone to talk, but it had never worked.

So now I was desperate. And I had resorted to the phone.

Only she wasn't answering. So I left a message.

Birdie has her own cell phone.

It's not for texting. It's for emergencies.

I figured this was sort of an emergency.

Then I used a messaging app on my iPad and typed a message there, too.

No response.

Next I called Mrs. Bhatt's cell phone since they don't have a landline. Only she didn't pick up either. I left a message asking Birdie to call me.

I told myself that with all of those messages, I would hear from Birdie soon. I just had to!

Right now, Mom was outside tying more planet balloons to the mailbox. Dad was in the kitchen getting all of the snacks prepared.

In the entranceway, Liam was all flushed and excited. Grandma Dort would say he was "on cloud nine," and I would say somewhere out in the stratosphere. That's the second layer of Earth's atmosphere.

I tried to pretend that I was up there in the stratosphere, too. Just thinking about happy-birthday thoughts and not about when I would hear from Birdie.

"It's like we stepped into a planetarium or something," I said. Before Liam was born, we had gone to the planetarium in Chicago. And in that dark, domed room, I had felt as if I were floating in outer space, visiting faraway constellations. Now it felt that way in our own home.

"Did you know that stars are like the hugest nuclear reactors ever?" I said. "That's because atoms split apart and release a ridiculous amount of energy."

Liam flexed his muscles. "I'm going to release a lot of energy at my party!" he cried.

"Yes, you sure will."

He studied my long-sleeved T-shirt. It said LIAM'S SPACE CREW for his birthday party. He had his own shirt that said SPACE COMMANDER. Mom had ordered them especially for today. "I can't wait for my party," he said.

Seeing him so pumped up lifted my mood. Everything was going to be perfect.

"Guess what?" said Liam. "I'm going to put up more stars in the bathroom."

"Great idea."

As he sprang away, I hung up some silver and black streamers. Meanwhile, I was listening hard, waiting for the phone to ring.

It didn't.

I tried to keep my mind on the birthday party. There were going to be so many activities for the kids.

Pin-the-tail-on-the-comet. Making moon phases with Oreos. Bobbing for planets. A piñata in the shape of Saturn.

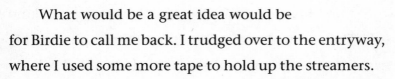

Then the phone rang. My heart leaped. I raced to get it. But Dad had already picked it up. I could hear him saying, "Yes, the party starts at eleven" and then "Great idea."

What would be a great idea would be for Birdie to call me back. I trudged over to the entryway, where I used some more tape to hold up the streamers.

A few minutes later, Liam sprinted toward me. "You got to see what I did. It looks soooo awesome. There's a planet in the bathroom."

"A planet? I don't remember the glow-in-the-dark kit coming with a planet."

"That's 'cause I made it myself." He waved a red Magic Marker in the air. "With this!" Sure enough, when I went over to check, on the bathroom wall next to the sink, he had scribbled what appeared to be the planet Mars.

Covering my mouth, I stifled a gasp. "Oh, Liam. Wow."

"It looks awesome, right?"

"It sure does." Somehow, I had to gently break the news to him. "I love how it's red just like Mars. But how will it come off?"

His face fell. "I didn't think about that."

"It's a cool idea, really. It's just that Mom and Dad had the bathroom painted, sort of recently. As in last summer. Remember?"

"No," he said in a small voice. "I mean, I guess, kind of." Then he made a cross between a harrumph and a big sigh. "Mom's going to be soooo mad. And Dad will say he's 'disappointed' in me."

"You don't know that," I said. When his little shoulders slumped, I felt awful.

"I knew today was going to be a bad luck day," he murmured.

"No, Liam, it's not." Although part of me thought that maybe it was. I paced. And paced some more. "There's got to be some way to fix this."

Then I thought about what Dr. Caroline might do. She has all of these cool demos and teaches you about what it's like to be a real scientist. She says, when you're stuck, get a little creative and get curious.

I, Kate Crawford, was definitely curious.

But I was also worried. Definitely worried.

Mom and Dad would check on us any minute now. I didn't want them to see Liam's very red and very big planet on those freshly painted mint-green walls. His party hadn't even started and things were already getting messy. Literally.

And Birdie hadn't called. Nothing was going right.

Guests were supposed to arrive in less than thirty minutes. Yikes. This wasn't looking good.

"Kate," said Liam. "You can fix it, right?"

"Um . . . yeah," I said, hoping I sounded more confident than I felt. I just had to figure out how. I could hear Mom opening the front door.

Okay, Kate, I told myself. *Stop panicking and take a deep breath. Ask yourself some questions. Get curious.*

So I wondered aloud, "What might break down the ink?"

"A magic wand?" said Liam.

"Nope," I said, getting an idea. "We don't need a wand. Not when we have a solvent. Because a solvent dissolves stuff." That's because of its chemical structure. From the cleaning closet, I grabbed a bottle of rubbing

alcohol and a clean rag. Onto the rag, I poured a splotch of rubbing alcohol. "Liam, you go for it. Rescue the walls. From the"—I tried to think of something appealing—"alien poison."

Lifting his hand over his head, he gave a champion salute. "I'll save the walls." He rubbed the scribbly looking planet, and then stared at the rag. "Hey, lookit! Now most of that alien poison is here."

"Good job, Liam! You did it."

If only it was that easy to clean up the mess with Birdie.

CHAPTER FIFTEEN

LiaM'S COMet

Occlusion (noun). In chemistry, this is what forms when you have one molecule within another. For example, that means you could find an impurity trapped inside a crystal. Guess you could no longer say it was crystal clear!

ABOUT TWENTY MINUTES LATER, the doorbell rang with the arrival of the first guest, a girl who was dressed like an astronaut. She looked awesome and carried a huge gift that Liam guessed was a spaceship model or a mini drum set. A steady flow of kids arrived, and the house grew louder and louder. Liam handed out alien antennae with silver Styrofoam balls for all of the kids to wear.

I still hadn't heard from Birdie.

HAPPY B

Soon, Mom had me helping with pin-the-tail-on-the-comet. I plonked some antennae on my head and then told the kids to line up. Naturally, I had the birthday boy go first. He placed the comet's streaky yellow tail all the way by the light switch. Then Desmond pinned the tail on our lamp. Another ended up on my elbow.

Spinning the kids and watching them dizzily trying to place the tail in the right place kept me distracted in a good kind of way. I explained that comets are made of rock, dust, ice, and gases.

"Does that mean that comets fart?" asked one boy with two missing front teeth.

"Well, they have plenty of sulfur," I said, plugging my nose. "So they're probably stinky." The kids starting giggling.

I was actually having fun, so when my watch alarm went off, I was surprised. It was time to get to the rocket

launch. And it looked like it would be without Birdie. I tried to ignore a sinking feeling in my stomach.

"My boots!" I cried aloud. I wanted to wear my pink cowboy boots. Rummaging through my closet, I couldn't find them anywhere.

After letting out a huff of frustration, I dove into my closet, throwing shoes, pushing past pants.

Oh, my boots were on a shelf. I slipped them on and instantly felt a little better.

Downstairs, I scooped up my bottle rocket and put on my winter coat. Then I grabbed our wagon from the garage, carefully placed my rocket on it, and called out, "Goodbye!" Of course, the house was noisy with birthday guests, so nobody could hear me. As fast as I could pull the wagon, I tore off down the street. Glancing at my watch, I saw that I was supposed to be on the field in ten minutes. If I jogged, I could make it there in time.

As I raced past our mailbox, with Liam's planet balloons, our elderly neighbor, Mrs. Schlesinger, was out getting the mail. "How's the party going?" she asked.

"Good!" I said, jogging down the sidewalk.

"Aren't you going in the wrong direction?" she asked.

"Yes!" I called out. "But I'll be right back. I'm going to the school."

"Be careful," she called out. "It's icy!"

"I will," I said.

Casting my eyes down, I scanned for black ice. Black ice forms on the surface of roads. And because it's transparent, it looks just like the road, only shinier. I read about how it has no trapped air bubbles, or occlusions. That's the science word for trapped bubbles in ice. Snow that's melting can get onto the sidewalks and become black ice when it refreezes. And then you can really slip.

I know this because I have done it like a thousand times.

And because my parents warn me about it every time I go outside.

With an eye out for black ice and giant cracks in the sidewalk, I ran as fast as I could. Looking at my watch,

I could see that the club was going to start Operation Rocket Launch in five minutes.

I jogged faster. Looking both ways, I crossed Brooke Avenue and made my way to the school, the red wagon clonking behind me.

Finally, I made it to the field with three minutes to spare. I spotted my friends: Elijah, Phoenix, Avery, Tala, and Memito. Even Jeremy. Plus, Skyler and Julia as well as a bunch of fourth graders. But no Birdie. What happened to her and where was she?

CHAPTER SIXTEEN

BLASTOFF!

Thermal energy (noun). This is energy in the form of heat. Basically, when the temperature rises, atoms move faster and bump into each other more frequently. Think of it like a fun game of bumper cars!

I PARKED THE WAGON ON THE SIDEWALK, scooped up my rocket, and raced to where everyone congregated on the field. Well, everyone except my best friend. I tried to push away my worried thoughts.

I had made it to the launch just in time.

Ms. Daly, who stood with her back to the gym, held up her watch. She was bundled up in a puffy

90

down jacket. "Glad you could make it, Kate," she said.

"Thanks," I said, breathless, as I set my rocket down next to Tala and Elijah. The tips of the grass were frosted. And I could see my breath in the air.

"It's so cold," said Elijah, squeezing his hands. "And I forgot to bring gloves."

"It's freezing," said Phoenix.

"I have an extra pair in my truck. I'll go get them," said Ms. Daly, and she ran off.

"We need to make some thermal energy," I said. "Like this!" Then I started doing jumping jacks.

Tala and Elijah joined me. "Hey, this is helping," said Elijah. Soon everyone in the club was doing jumping jacks.

"Where's Birdie?" he asked.

"I don't know," I admitted.

"Is something wrong?" He looked concerned. "I mean, between you guys?"

"No," I said. At least, from my point of view, nothing was wrong. Except that I was worried.

"I really don't want to talk about it," I snapped.

"Okay, sorry," said Elijah, and I immediately felt bad for being grumpy. But I couldn't help it. Because most of

91

all I hoped that Birdie was okay. But if she wasn't okay, she would let me know. Eventually. I swallowed hard. Maybe a family thing came up? She has a huge extended family and they get together a lot since a bunch of them live in Michigan. Maybe one of her cousins had another baby or something and she forgot to tell me.

Ms. Daly returned with the extra pair of gloves and handed them to Elijah, who told her he actually wasn't cold anymore. "Because of thermal energy."

"Me neither," I said, breathless.

"Yay!" said Tala, and she started to shake, shimmy, and do her happy dance. We all joined in, including Ms. Daly. When we were all toasty, Ms. Daly said it was launch time.

"Pilots often talk to their planes before a flight," said Ms. Daly, who sometimes told us stories of her days in the air force. "They'll speak aloud to their planes and say things like "Take care of me." So before you launch, I'd like everyone to talk to their rockets."

Some of the kids started to giggle. I tried to smile, too.

"Hey, it's a tradition," said Ms. Daly. "I'd advise that you say something nice."

"You better go higher than Memito's rocket," said Elijah to his rocket. "And Jeremy's."

"You better go to the moon," said Memito to his rocket.

"You better prepare to lose the race," said Jeremy to his rocket.

I felt too upset to say anything to my rocket, so I sort of petted it like it was Dribble.

"Some pilots won't point at the sky because they believe it will cause bad weather," said Ms. Daly. "But we all know that bad weather is caused by a low-pressure system."

Phew. I was secretly glad that Ms. Daly didn't believe in superstitious stuff like that. "But I've seen pilots give a big ole hug to the nose of their plane," she continued. "So feel free to give your nose a little hug, too." She grinned.

"Nose?" asked Memito.

I pointed to the cone of the rocket. "This is the nose."

"Oh, right! I forgot." Memito shook his head. "I'm not hugging it or kissing it," he said. "No way!"

Meanwhile Avery and Phoenix were hugging their

noses. I looked to see if Birdie had finally made it to the field. But I didn't see her anywhere. Maybe her cousin really did have a baby?

"Does everyone have their cork with  them?" asked Tala, who had popped up to stand next to Ms. Daly. "Because you need something to seal your bottle." She held up a cork. "Does anyone need a new cork?"

Julia raised her hand.

"There you go." Ms. Daly handed her an extra cork. "Now remember, if the cork is too loose, it will fall out. Shake, shake, shake your bottle to test to see if it will stay in."

Julia shook and the cork tumbled out. Her face fell.

"Oooops," she said.

"That's okay," said Ms. Daly. "We can fix it. With a bit of tape, you can wrap it around the cork until it's a bit bigger, and then you'll get a nice and tight fit. And you'll be ready to launch. I've got some extra tape in my car. I'll go and get it."

"Thanks," called out Julia. "That would be great."

"Tala can help you while I get the tape," said Ms. Daly, who started to dash back to the parking lot.

Tala gave a thumbs-up. "Let me know if you need any assistance getting set up."

For a moment, I felt just a tiny bit jealous. Ugh. My emotions were all over the place today. Usually I'm the one who gets to explain things in chemistry club. But really, I was mostly glad for Tala. After all, it was cool how much she knew about rockets. And as the new girl, she was really fitting in super quick. Almost as if she could read my mind, she called my name. "Kate, can you help me explain a little bit about the chemistry of these rockets?"

"Absolutely!" I zipped over to Tala. "So here's the deal with our rocket 'fuel.'" I pointed to the plastic bottles of white vinegar on a card table. "You've got the acetic acid, what we call vinegar, over there and you need to pour it into your bottle. Then we add the sodium bicarbonate—the baking soda. When vinegar and baking soda mix together, you get a chemical reaction and it produces carbon dioxide. You'll know your rocket is working when you start to see some fizzing."

Tala clapped her hands. "Thanks, Kate. Once you've filled up your bottle halfway with vinegar, you're going to drop in your toilet-paper packet of baking soda, put in the cork, and then move away from the rocket fast. I'm going to demonstrate first with my bottle rocket. And then you all can do it, too." She pointed to the jugs of vinegar. "Everyone, if you haven't already, fill up your rocket with acetic acid."

Along with other kids, I raced over and filled up my rocket.

"Got your fuel pack?" asked Tala.

"Yes," kids chorused, pulling the packets out of their pockets. Ms. Daly waved at us as she emerged from the parking lot with the tape. She soon handed it to Julia, who looked grateful.

"Yay!" I said, trying my best to be cheerful. "I'm glad you're not going to miss out on the big launch."

"Thanks," she said

Opening up the cap, Tala squeezed in her packet, added the cork, and then bolted from the rocket. I scooted away along with everyone else. "Okay, is everyone ready to start counting?"

A chorus of voices, including mine, chanted, "Yes!"

At that moment Tala glanced down at her watch.

And that's when I looked at my watch. I couldn't believe the time.

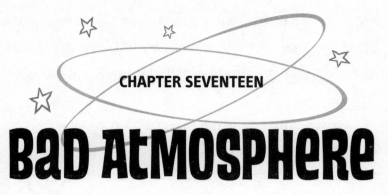

CHAPTER SEVENTEEN

BaD AtMOSPHeRe

Atmospheric particles (noun). These are teeny-tiny particles (like dust) suspended in the air. And guess what? Snowflakes form when super-cold water droplets freeze onto these particles. particles. So even though particles are small, they can have mighty jobs to do.

IT WAS 12:25. I was supposed to leave at 12:15 to pick up Liam's ice cream cake. But I had forgotten to reset the alarm on my watch.

My rocket was ready, but it didn't matter; I had to leave.

"Got to go!" I yelled.

"But your rocket!" Tala pointed at my packet of fuel. "It's all ready to go now."

"You can do it for me. Take a video!" I shouted. "I'll meet you guys at Brewster's in a bit. I've got to get to my brother's birthday party." *And pick up the cake.* But I didn't say that part. There really wasn't time to explain. At the edge of the parking lot, I grabbed my wagon and bolted.

On the field, I heard the chemistry club members counting down, "Ten, nine, eight . . ." and I thought about how I had my own countdown.

"Three, two, one. Blastoff!" everyone shouted.

Turning my head, I watched in awe as the rockets fizzed and whooshed upward! Kids whooped, clapped, and cheered. The rockets soared straight up, going well over the two-story school before arcing back down. It was an amazing sight. But I didn't feel as happy as I should have.

The sun slid behind a cloud. The wind picked up, and the sky took on a pink hue, the way it does before the flurries come down. I learned from Dr. Caroline that light bouncing off clouds and particles is scattered. This means that we can see longer wavelengths of color, like pink.

Usually, I loved pink. My cowboy boots I was wearing were pink.

My quilt had pink in it.

But I didn't want a pink snow-sky because that meant trouble. And there was already enough of it today.

No. No. Nooooo. Not a snowstorm, too. I charged past some older Victorian houses by the school. They looked like dollhouses, with their towers, turrets, and wraparound porches. If Birdie were with me, she'd slow down and get a dreamy look on her face. Like she wanted to shrink the houses and put one in her bedroom. That was what she'd done when we were younger, when she still played with stuffed animals and dolls.

I flew past the little cemetery where Birdie always holds her breath. Because she says it's a thing you're supposed to do. Right now, I would do anything if she could be with me. Somehow, she'd make me feel calmer.

Glancing down at my watch, I noted with horror that it was already 12:29. Just one minute to get to McSweeny's, and it was ten blocks away.

If I were on my bike, I could get there in five minutes.

If I were in a spaceship, I'd already be there.

The wagon clunked over pebbles on the sidewalk

and chunks of ice. I navigated along the narrow path on the sidewalk as fast as I could go.

I imagined myself on the soccer field in the spring, running with my coach yelling at us during warm-ups around the field. I pushed myself to go faster and faster until suddenly, I was sliding.

Black ice. No. No. No.

I started to tumble down, but I was able to grab on to a mailbox for balance. My head slammed against the mailbox but thankfully not too hard. Standing back up, I brushed myself off and blinked away the pain.

I'm fine, I told myself. *Just fine.*

And there across the street was the ice cream store on the corner. McSweeny's looked dark, like nobody was there. But Mr. Arvanites was known for not turning on the lights. "Natural sunlight," he would say. "Good for your skin. And saves electric bills."

When I reached the store, I noticed a sign that said CLOSED.

And there was a note stuck on the door.

Waited 10 minutes but had to run to the dentist. Be back in 2 hours. Should still be more than enough time for you to have cake after dinner!

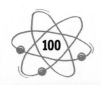

100

Dinner! This cake was supposed to be for right after lunch! I could feel tears welling up.

No. No. No.

Somehow, I had once again messed up my brother's birthday. Not because he was born on December thirteenth. But because he got me as a sister. I was bad luck. My face, even in the cold, felt hot. My throat closed up.

I plopped on the stoop of the ice cream store, my head in my hands. At that moment, I realized something that was quantifiable, observable, and true.

I was the worst sister in the entire world.

I let my brother down. I let my new friend down. And I didn't even get a chance to launch my rocket.

This was the worst day ever.

CHAPTER EIGHTEEN

EMPtY-HaNDED

Molecules (noun). These are microscopic units of a substance. So a water molecule is the smallest piece of matter that is still, well, water. Even though, with our eyes, we might not be able to see the water molecules that have boiled off a pot of water, you can imagine them having an invisible dance party floating around in the air as steam!

I STARED AT MY EMPTY WAGON and my empty, scraped-up hands.

What a total failure.

I wanted to melt into the nearby snowbank.

And then I thought about something I had learned in science. Was a glass beaker actually empty? No. It was filled with air. Air was made up of molecules. From a scientific point of view, the beaker was filled to the brim.

102

Just like outer space wasn't really empty either, but filled with stuff like particles and plasma, dust and cosmic rays.

I guess from a scientific point of view, I wasn't actually empty-handed. Bending down, I examined my palm and rubbed my chilly fingers. They were bleeding a little bit, and freezing, since I hadn't had time to slip on my gloves.

What was I going to do?

I couldn't say, "Hey, Liam. Sorry, I was too late to pick up your special ice cream cake," then cup my hands and say, "But here, have some air instead. There's plenty of molecules in there to keep you busy until your next birthday."

No. That definitely wouldn't work.

My fingers were freezing from the cold. My head stung from my fall. My throat was dry from running. And, somehow, underneath my winter jacket I was sweating, too. There was no doubt about it. I was going to let Liam down.

Again.

I felt terrible. Like how a balloon looks if you put it in the freezer after you blow it up. All small and wrinkled and useless.

I studied the pavement, trying to figure out the best way to apologize. Suddenly, I heard a honk. When I looked up, I saw Birdie and her mom and sister in their SUV. They eased to a stop in front of me.

Birdie rolled down her window from the back of the SUV. "Kate, are you okay?" she asked.

"I'm fine," I said, because I didn't want to be a burden.

"You're not fine," said Mrs. Bhatt in her usual no-nonsense but warm style. It was probably why she won so many cases as a trial lawyer.

"You're right," I said. "Everything is messed up." I sniffed hard to hold back tears.

"I knew it," said Birdie. "I told Mom to stop. We were on the way to the library."

"Sure are," said Meela, Birdie's older sister. She held up a heavy stack of fantasy novels.

I blinked and stared. "I tried to call you. And you weren't at the rocket launch, so I was worried. On top of everything else."

"What else?" asked Birdie softly.

"I'm a mess-up." I sniffed and then quickly explained what had just happened.

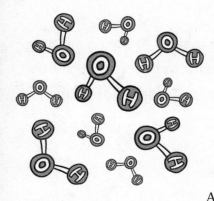

"You're anything but a mess-up," declared Birdie. "You're Kate. You love science, especially chemistry, and you make it fun. You love soccer and penguins. And your family."

Suddenly, I didn't feel quite so deflated anymore. I felt more than a little hopeful. At least when it came to Birdie. But not about anything else. I let out a deep sigh.

"My family's going to be so disappointed. A galaxy of disappointment, especially Liam."

"Um, are you suffering from hypothermia? Because the Kate Crawford I know does not give up."

"Maybe you're right," I said.

"Didn't you make astronaut ice cream when you did your report on the Apollo 11 mission for social studies last year?"

Wait a minute. I did.

"So, you have the equipment," said Birdie.

"Oh my gosh. We have the liquid nitrogen. Dad was even using it right outside the garage to make the cloudy atmosphere on Jupiter."

"So that means you can make astronaut ice cream for Liam. Remember those delicious little frozen chunks you made in class? He'll love it. I know I did. The ice cream was delicious."

"Birdie, you're a genius!" I said.

"I know that," said Mrs. Bhatt.

"And me too," said Meela, lifting her head out of her book.

Then I grabbed the handle of my wagon. "I've got to get home!"

"Throw your wagon in the trunk and we'll take you home," said Mrs. Bhatt.

"Thank you," I said. "Thank you so much." Soon my eyes met Birdie's as I sat next to her in the back seat.

Birdie was quiet again. I lowered my voice. "Is everything okay with Meela?" I gestured toward her sister, whose head was once again buried in a novel. Next to Meela, Mrs. Bhatt bopped to the beat of an oldie rock song as she drove.

"My sister?" Birdie whispered. "What do you mean?"

"You had to do something secret with her last week," I reminded her in a whisper. "Is she okay?"

"It didn't really have anything to do with my sister,"

said Birdie, lowering her voice more, even though there was no way her sister could hear us over the music. "It was Tala."

"What about her?"

"I guess I was sort of jealous," Birdie said. "It started when you let her draw your tattoo instead of me. I felt dumped or something. And then you couldn't even figure out why I was upset. It felt like you didn't even know me anymore."

"Oh my gosh, Birdie. No, you're my best friend. Forever and ever. Nobody could replace you. You seemed super busy with your parrot tattoo, and Tala happened to make an atom. And I just thought it was cool." I placed my hand over my heart. "Seriously. You know you're my bestie. And I'm really sorry I didn't figure out why you were upset. I didn't even think you'd be upset about that! I promise next time you can draw my tattoo. You're the best artist I know. But I do like Tala. And I hope all three of us can be friends." I paused. "Or at least I can be friends with both of you at the same time."

"I'm sorry, too," said Birdie. "I just worried that you didn't like me as much anymore."

"Not possible."

"I know. And, Kate, I think I'd like to get to know Tala, too."

"That would be awesome," I said just as we pulled up to my house.

"I've got an idea," said Birdie. "And I think you might really like it."

"What?" I said. "Tell me."

"You'll see," said Birdie.

"I can't take any more not knowing stuff."

Birdie put her arm around me. "I'm going to go with you to the party. Together, we'll help make the best astronaut ice cream in the entire world."

CHAPTER NINETEEN

Hot and Cold

Chemical bond (noun). This is the force that holds two atoms together. There are different kinds of bonds, and they can be broken and re-formed. Think of it like a bunch of kids holding hands playing Red Rover. They let go of each other's hands and sometimes find new partners.

WHEN BIRDIE AND I WALKED INTO MY HOUSE, it was oddly quiet. No loud screaming or thundering feet of twenty kindergartners slamming into furniture.

"They must be eating," I said as we headed into the kitchen.

Sure enough, Liam sat with his friends at a long folding metal table draped in a tablecloth dotted with planets. The boys and girls were finishing up their lunch, which were little pizza bagels that looked like flying

saucers. There were also slices of lunchmeat cut into the shape of crescent moons and stars.

"Hi!" I said. "I'm back!"

"Yay!" cried a bunch of kids.

A girl with two small pigtails shouted, "Spin me, Kate!"

"And me!" cried Liam.

"Well, not right now," said Dad, who was by the fridge filling up a pitcher with more water. "Since you all need to finish your lunch so we can eat ice cream cake."

"Cake!" Liam cried, and my heart sank.

"Cake! Cake! Cake!" the rest of the kids chanted along with him.

I looked at Birdie, and she looked at me.

"I can't wait to see this masterpiece," said Mom, who was wearing a SPACE CREW T-shirt just like me and Dad.

I bit my bottom lip. "Well, about that. You

will see the cake. But just a little later." Then I explained how I had just missed Mr. Arvanites and that we could pick up the cake before dinner.

"No ice cream cake for my party?" asked Liam, his voice wobbling. He blinked, and I was afraid he would start to cry.

"Actually, you will still have ice cream. But it won't be a cake. Instead, you will have . . . astronaut ice cream," I announced.

A bunch of kids, and my parents, stared at me in amazement and confusion.

"Using some awesome chemistry skills," I said in my most enthusiastic voice, "we're going to make futuristic astronaut ice cream. With liquid nitrogen."

There was silence, and then suddenly the room erupted into cheers.

My mom raised her eyebrows in concern. "Kate, are you really sure about this?"

"She did make ice cream last year for her project," said Dad.

"Oh, I'm very sure," I said. "Let's get ready. Because it's time for the coolest ice cream ever!"

"At least we've done this one before," said Dad. "I'll

go grab the liquid nitrogen from the garage. Operation Make the Atmosphere of Jupiter was a huge success, and we have plenty of liquid nitrogen left over."

"See?" whispered Birdie. "It's all working out."

"It is," I agreed.

Soon enough Dad, wearing his safety goggles and gloves, came back with the dewar of liquid nitrogen. A dewar is an awesome vacuum-insulated container that keeps the liquid nitrogen nice and cold so that it doesn't boil away.

"So, everyone, nitrogen is usually a gas," I explained, "but when it's chilled under high pressure, it becomes a cold liquid. And when I say 'cold,' I mean arctic cold. That's why we need to be super safe."

"With these." Dad pointed to the safety goggles he was wearing with one of his blue cryogenic gloves. Those are special gloves that scientists wear to protect their hands from extreme temperatures.

"It's important to be careful since the liquid nitrogen is negative one hundred and ninety-six degrees Celsius," said Mom, who helped me grab ingredients for the ice cream: whole milk, sugar, salt, chocolate syrup, mint extract, and vanilla. Plus mixing bowls, measuring cups, and spoons. "So nobody can touch that dewar of liquid nitrogen," added Mom.

"Not even us," I added as I ran to grab goggles and gloves from the basement. Birdie was already retrieving our matching blue lab coats from the mud room.

After putting on my safety equipment, I set the two mixing bowls on the counter, one for me, one for Birdie. I also pre-measured out one cup of sugar for each of us. Luckily, we had two sets of measuring cups.

"It's going to be incredible," gushed Birdie. "Wait till you astronauts taste all of the little crunchy shapes."

"I scream, you scream, we all scream for ice cream," shouted Dad.

The kids all started screaming, with Liam yelling the loudest.

"Thanks, Dad," I joked. Putting my fingers to my lips, I motioned for them to be quiet. The hollering and cheering continued.

"No ice cream until you're quiet," said Birdie.

Suddenly, there was silence.

Mom gave Birdie a thumbs-up. "You could become a principal someday if you wanted," she said.

"Okay, everyone, we're going to have some fun with chemistry," I announced. "All of you are about to eat astronaut ice cream." I turned to Dad and Birdie. "You guys ready?"

"Oh yeah," said Birdie, who, just like me, stood in front of giant blue mixing bowls.

"First thing we need to do is add the sugar," I said, and both Birdie and I dumped our sugar into our bowls.

Next we added in two tablespoons of vanilla. "This will spike it with flavor," I said.

Birdie bent down and smelled her mixture. "Mmmm, yummy."

I held up mint extract. "In mine, I'm squirting one teaspoon of mint extract. So we'll have options. Vanilla and mint astronaut ice cream."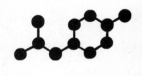

And then I grabbed the carton of salt. "Where's our birthday boy?"

Liam jumped up. "I'm here!"

I poured some salt into my cupped hand. "Take a pinch, Liam, and toss some into both bowls."

Liam dramatically pinched his fingers together. "I'm a space lobster!" he cried.

"Just don't be a greedy lobster. Then you'll be shell-fish," Birdie joked.

After I stopped giggling, I explained to everyone why you needed to add salt. "It lowers the freezing point," I said. "That allows the milk mixture to get nice and cold without freezing, which is what we need for ice cream. Right now, I want everyone to make a giant whoop if you are ready to get started."

"Whoop whoop!" the kids cried.

"And now we're going to add a third of a gallon of whole milk. It has to be whole milk. None of that low-fat stuff." I made a silly face as Mom handed me the gallon of whole milk and I poured a third of a gallon into each bowl. "We need the fat to give the ice cream its *creamy* texture. Otherwise, the sugar-milk mixture would turn into a giant iceberg when it interacts with the liquid nitrogen."

"Can we eat the ice cream now?" lisped a girl with one missing front tooth.

"Almost! We need to get all of the ingredients mixed

together and then add the liquid nitrogen so our ice cream gets super cold," I said. "All of this just takes a little teamwork and cooperation."

"It's time to stir, right?" asked Birdie, picking up her big mixing spoon.

I tapped my spoon against the bowl. "Yup, stir, stir, stir. It's important to get all that sugar to dissolve. Everyone move your arm and pretend to stir with us." The kids all mimed stirring, some of them wiggling like they were doing a stirring dance. Birdie and I couldn't help giggling.

"Okay." I nodded at Dad. "It's time."

"Liquid nitrogen is very, very cold," said Dad.

"So stand back, everyone," added Mom. "We don't want to get it on anyone."

Even though Birdie and I had on our lab coats, goggles, and gloves, we also took a huge step back. "Safety first," I said.

Dad poured in the liquid nitrogen, and for a moment, the whole area clouded up.

"It's just like the atmosphere on Jupiter," cried Liam.

"Or Venus or Saturn," cried another kid. It was true. Puffs of what looked like fog hovered over the counter.

"Isn't this amazing?" I called out. "Okay, even though it's hard to see the bowls, Birdie and I are stir-stir-stirring right now. So I want you all to do the same with your pretend spoons."

I mixed everything around as much as I could until the texture felt a bit gravelly. It looked lumpy and bumpy and perfect.

"It's ready!" I said, glancing at Birdie's bowl of vanilla.

"Yup!" said Birdie.

"Grab spoons, everyone, and bowls. Real ones. Not imaginary."

Liam was first in line. I scooped him up some vanilla and mint, and handed him the chocolate syrup. "Here you go, buddy!"

After dumping half the bottle on his ice cream, he spooned some into his mouth. "Yummy!" He turned to his friend Desmond. "See, thirteen isn't a bad number. 'Cause I've got thirteen pieces of astronaut ice cream."

"I want thirteen pieces, too," said Desmond, nodding eagerly.

117

The rest of the kids, including Desmond, lined up and requested thirteen pieces of ice cream. Afterward, we sang "Happy Birthday," and there were lots of cheeks streaked with chocolate and vanilla.

"I love astronaut ice cream," said Liam. "Can we do this again?"

"Yes," I cried. "Only next time, let's do different flavors. Maybe we could try mango extract. Or cotton candy!"

"My tummy is happy," said Liam.

"Mine too," I said. "Your stomach is one of the places where your body breaks down food for energy and nutrients. All of that happens through chemical reactions. Which is just a way of saying one substance is changed into a completely different one."

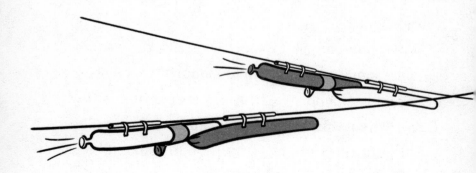

That means it's about change.

And change is always exciting. Even if it can be, well, surprising.

And maybe even sort of fun. "Now we're going to do double balloon rockets," I said with a huge grin.

We all went to the table where I had all of the supplies. "Okay, everyone, grab your balloons. We're about to blast off for the space station."

Soon enough the kids were having a blast with their balloon rockets whizzing and whirring all over the family room. Liam and Desmond kept crisscrossing their fishing line in an attempt to try to create the ultimate rocket collision by our fish tank. I couldn't help but smile. Even the fish were amused by the event. I might have missed my own launch, but this one was awesome in its own way.

"Hey, guys, I've got to meet back up with the chemistry club at Brewster's." I leaned over to Birdie and whispered, "For hot chocolate and s'mores."

"Do you want us to save you some astronaut ice cream?" asked Mom. "It turns out we have an extra bowl."

"That would be awesome," I said.

"Can I come with you?" Birdie asked.

"Yes," I said. "I'd really like that."

"Hey, you're still wearing your party T-shirt," said Liam.

"Oops!" I dashed upstairs to change and brush my hair.

When I came back down, Birdie was leading the kids in a chorus of "Five Little Planets Jumping in Outer Space."

CHAPTER TWENTY

SOMETHING SWEET

Melting point (noun). This is the temperature at which a solid will melt. The melting point of chocolate is between 86°F and 90°F. Which is definitely the sweet spot. Especially when it comes to a chocolate bar melting with the gooey marshmallow on your graham cracker.

THIS TIME WHEN I STROLLED along the sidewalk, even though the sky was still pink and looked like maybe it would snow, I didn't mind. Because I'd just made the best mint-flavored astronaut ice cream. And I'd finally been able to reconnect with my BFF.

"I'm so glad you're coming," I said.

"Me too," she said. "For a little bit, I thought maybe

you didn't like me anymore because I was boring. That I didn't know anything about outer space. That maybe art wasn't cool."

"Are you kidding? Did you know that the first person to ever do a spacewalk was also an artist? Tala told me about him. His name was Alexei Leonov. After his spacewalk, his pressure suit inflated and he spun uncontrollably, yet Alexei miraculously got back to the airlock safely. Then, when he was hurling back to Earth in a cramped little capsule, he created the first piece of art in space. He tied colored pencils to a piece of string to prevent them from floating around the capsule and sketched an image of the sunrise. It looked like a rainbow curving over the world."

"That's so cool," said Birdie.

"Yeah," I said.

"Sometimes art and science are the same thing," said Birdie.

"Sometimes." I stared at the lovely pink sky. "By the way, thanks for saving me back there. I mean it. You know me so well. Remembering the astronaut ice cream was perfect. I should have thought of it, though."

"That's what best friends are for," whispered Birdie. "To remember things."

We walked in silence for a few minutes before Birdie exclaimed, "Look!" She pointed upward, and I could see flurries drifting from the sky.

"I knew it. The pink sky." And I explained how the light changes before it snows.

"Of course you would know that," said Birdie.

"Sometimes we know different things," I said.

She nodded.

"That's a good thing."

She nodded some more.

When we got to Brewster's, all the kids from the chemistry club and Ms. Daly were there.

"Take a seat at a table," said Ms. Daly. "With our club treasury, I ordered everyone hot chocolates. Oh, and there's s'mores to be made."

"Awesome," I said.

"I'm sorry you missed the rocket launch," she said. "It was a great success."

"That's okay." Then I explained how I had launched double balloon rockets at home as part of my brother's party.

That's when Elijah, Memito, and Jeremy waved to us. I thought about sitting with them. But instead we slid in with Phoenix, Avery, and Tala. I wanted Tala and Birdie to have some time together.

Soon enough, a waitress brought over hot chocolate. And there were already all the fixings for s'mores—graham crackers, chocolates, and marshmallows. In the middle of the stone table sat a mini firepit/Bunsen burner thing that was powered by propane. Another example of chemistry in action!

As I toasted my marshmallow on a little metal stick over the flame, I nudged Tala. "Hey, I told Birdie about the Alexei guy. You know, the first person ever to do a spacewalk. And how he was an artist."

"That sounds so awesome," said Birdie. "I could totally see that as a graphic novel."

"What? Same here," said Tala. "I love graphic novels."

"I do, too," said Birdie, and soon they were wrapped up in a conversation about their favorites.

I couldn't help smiling. Seeing them chatting like that was the best. Plus, I was about to make the perfect s'more. It was a scientific fact. Once my marshmallow got toasty brown but not burned, the crisp outer shell combined with the soft inside made the best combination on the planet. I smushed my gooey marshmallow onto the graham cracker and gave it a second to melt the chocolate, before popping it into my mouth.

"Mmmm," I said. "So good."

Elijah came over. "I like your birthday shirt."

"What?" I looked down and saw that it said LIAM'S SPACE CREW.

"Oh no! I somehow forgot to change out of it." I had been so focused on brushing some ice cream out of my hair that I'd completely forgotten about my shirt.

"It's cool," said Elijah.

Honestly, I breathed a sigh of relief that it was the only thing that actually ended up going wrong today.

Well, that and the fact that we still had to pick up Liam's cake later on this evening.

I thought about how today got a little bit mixed up and how it wasn't so bad. Life is a lot like chemistry. When you mix things up, everything changes. Sometimes—like with astronaut ice cream—mixing things together makes it taste even sweeter.

DOUBLE BALLOON ROCKET

MATERIALS:

☆ 2 long balloons (like for balloon animals)
☆ 2 wide straws
☆ 2 light clamps (or binder clips)
☆ Fishing line (30–40 feet)
☆ Cardboard roll from a paper towel or toilet paper tube
☆ Clear tape
☆ Balloon pump
☆ Scissors
☆ A table

PROTOCOL:

1. Have an adult help you tie one side of the fishing line to a high corner of the room.

2. String the fishing line through the first straw [STRAW 1].

3. String the fishing line through the second straw [STRAW 2].

4. Tie the other end of the fishing line to an object in the lower corner on the opposite side of the room. Make sure the line is stretched tight!

5. Cut a 1-inch ring from the cardboard roll.

6. Inflate one balloon, but do not tie it.

7. Thread the open end of BALLOON 1 through the

cardboard ring, without letting the balloon deflate. The cardboard ring should fit around BALLOON 1 tightly.

8. Clamp the end of BALLOON 1 shut.

9. Place the balloon/ring apparatus on a table. Place the clamped side of BALLOON 1 on the right side of the table.

10. Inflate the second balloon [BALLOON 2], but do not tie it.

11. Starting from the left side of the cardboard ring, carefully thread the unclamped tip of BALLOON 2 through the ring without letting the balloon deflate. This will not be easy; take your time to push or pull the balloon tip until it appears on the right side of the cardboard ring.

12. Clamp BALLOON 2 shut.

13. Pull the cardboard ring down to the bottom six inches of BALLOON 1.

14. Point the clamped ends of the balloons toward the higher corner of the room. Carefully tape the cardboard ring to the lowest side of STRAW 1. Use another piece of tape to secure the highest side of STRAW 1 to BALLOON 1.

15. Use tape to secure the end of BALLOON 2 to STRAW 2.

16. Move the balloon rocket to the high corner of the room.

17. Quickly remove the clamp from the first balloon, then the second balloon, and watch the rocket propel across the room!

HOW It WORKS:

Our Double Balloon Rocket acts just like rockets that go into space! The first balloon is the most important, because it is the one that is used to get the rocket moving.

It releases air to push the rocket along the fishing line; the air molecules move out of the balloon in one direction, making the rocket move in the opposite direction. As soon as the first balloon has deflated, it detaches from the second balloon, triggering the second balloon to begin deflating. Our rocket finally stops moving once all of the air molecules have been released from the two balloons. What would happen if we added a third balloon to our model? Would the rocket be able to move faster? Farther?

DR. Kate Biberdorf, also known as Kate the Chemist by her fans, is a science professor at UT–Austin by day and a science superhero by night (well, she does that by day, too). Kate travels the country building a STEM army of kids who love science as much as she does. You can often find her breathing fire or making slime—always in her lab coat and goggles.

You can visit Kate on Instagram and Facebook @KatetheChemist, on Twitter @K8theChemist, and online at KatetheChemist.com.

DON'T MISS ALL OF KATE'S ADVENTURES!

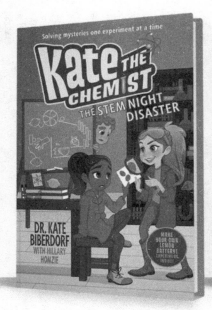

Become a scientist lik

Kate the Chemist!